I0587818

MURDER AT THE RACES

A ROSA REED MYSTERY BOOK 6

LEE STRAUSS
NORM STRAUSS

la plume PRESS

Copyright © 2021 by Lee Strauss

Cover by Steven Novak

Cover Illustration by Amanda Sorenson

All rights reserved.

No part of this book may be reproduced in any form or by any electronic or mechanical means, including information storage and retrieval systems, without written permission from the author, except for the use of brief quotations in a book review.

Library and Archives Canada Cataloguing in Publication

Library and Archives Canada Cataloguing in Publication

Title: Murder at the Races / Lee Strauss.

Names: Strauss, Lee (Novelist), author.

Description: Series statement: A Rosa Reed mystery ; 6 | "A 1950s cozy historical mystery."

Identifiers: Canadiana (print) 2020029802X | Canadiana (ebook) 20200298046 | ISBN 9781774091425

(hardcover) | ISBN 978-1-77409-159-3 (softcover) | ISBN 9781774091418 (IngramSpark softcover) | ISBN

9781774091388 (Kindle) | ISBN 9781774091395 (EPUB)

Classification: LCC PS8637.T739 M874 2021 | DDC C813/.6—dc23

*N*ASCAR had come to Santa Bonita and it was all the Forrester family could talk about. Newly established in California from London, England, Rosa Reed was thrilled to be going to a stock car race for the first time in her life.

Aunt Louisa, ever elegant with her freshly dyed, backcombed-high chestnut hair—tips flipped at her shoulders—sipped on a steaming cup of coffee as they sat around the breakfast table overlooking the pool and the luxurious gardens. "I've heard these events are absolutely thunderous! I am not sure I am looking forward to the smell of gasoline and dust." Her involvement in the town's charity events, including this one, was renowned.

Clarence cast a glance at his mother over the

morning paper. "The track is asphalt, Mom. It will be loud, but not that dusty." Dressed in a plain white T-shirt and loose-fitting denim pants, he hadn't yet applied his Brylcreem hair product, making his look unruly and tousled.

Rosa wasn't the only one to note her cousin's uncharacteristic unkempt appearance.

"You're looking a bit messy today, Clarence." Although her tone was a tad snide, the corners of Gloria's mouth pulled back in a taunting smile. Though a few years younger than her brother, Gloria and Clarence could be mistaken for twins with their dark hair and tanned good looks. "Does forfeiting a hair comb make you drive faster?"

Glancing at Rosa, Gloria giggled. Clarence had a serious, sometimes brooding personality, and Rosa, rather unsportingly, enjoyed listening to her free-spirited younger cousin tease him.

"Well, ring-a-ding ding," Clarence shot back.

Gloria sniffed playfully. "No need to get all frosted."

Rosa raised a brow at the baffling slang her cousins used but thought it wise to stay out of the fray.

"We have to wear helmets," Clarence explained, the annoyance clear in his tone. "No use in getting the jelly roll all perfect when you have to wear headgear."

Rosa hid her grin with one palm. *Jelly roll?*

"I am glad you're wearing a helmet," Aunt Louisa said. "There are a lot of mishaps in those races. And remember, you have a daughter."

Five-year-old Julie was Clarence's only child and was spending the weekend with her mother, Vanessa. Rosa doubted that Vanessa and Julie would be attending the race. The divorce had not been amicable.

"Yeah, there are some crashes," Clarence admitted, "but injuries are fairly rare. We are strapped in pretty tight."

"Yes, but you have a tendency to bite off more than you can chew," Aunt Louisa commented. "You don't always behave responsibly."

The brooding expression on Clarence's face deepened into a scowl as he continued to read the paper. Rosa felt bad for him. While Gloria's teasing was usually innocent, Aunt Louisa's remarks towards him tended to be more disparaging.

Rosa caught Clarence's eye. "I think it's very exciting."

"If you find death exciting," Gloria said, her gaze

narrowed on her brother. "Aren't there professional drivers in this race?"

"A few. But I'm not trying to win against them. I just want to put in a good showing and have some kicks."

"And help to raise money," Rosa added.

Clarence finished the last gulp of his orange juice and stood to leave. "Right, that too."

Gloria sipped her coffee, a renewed tension showing on her face. Rosa patted her arm. "You're going to do great."

"I'm just so nervous," Gloria admitted. "It's my first real assignment, and I don't want to mess things up. Jake Wilson will never let me live it down."

Gloria, a journalism student, had recently got an intern position at *The Santa Bonita Morning Star*. Unfortunately, the person she was to shadow was an arrogant young reporter with the annoying habit of praising Gloria's looks as he demeaned her intelligence.

"Never mind Mr. Wilson," Rosa said. "You don't work for him."

"That's *right*," Gloria said, a new determination on her face. "I'm freelancing. I work for myself."

"Well, girls," Aunt Louisa said as she pushed away from the table. "I'm going to ready myself for this afternoon's festivities, and I suggest you do the same."

Rosa returned to her spacious bedroom. All the Forrester mansion rooms were vast, making even the impressive rooms of Hartigan House—her childhood home in South Kensington—feel small. She practically swam among the satin sheets of her king-size four-poster bed. A mound of fluffy pillows partially hid the headboard, and her small gray tabby cat curled at the foot.

Rosa scratched the cat's ears and kissed his soft forehead. "Oh, Diego. You're such a cutie patootie."

As if he couldn't decide if the moniker pleased or annoyed him, Diego blinked back slowly.

Outside the large windows, the sun shone brightly, and a light breeze caught the fronds of the palm trees, causing them to dance lightly. So much sun and sunlight, and for November! Rosa missed her parents mightily, but the drizzly wet of England? Never.

Approaching her built-in closet, another delightful American invention, Rosa selected a short-sleeve, fine-knit, fitted sweater top in pink. She knotted a matching neck scarf, angling it to the left side. Black capri pants, matching ballet-style slip-on shoes, and a wide-brimmed straw hat to shade her face, completed her outfit—perfectly suited for the races.

Music from Gloria's radio filtered down the hall. The station played hits from the forties, and when Doris Day singing "Sentimental Journey" came on, it immediately pulled Rosa back in time to a school dance she had attended in 1945.

Though born and raised in London, Rosa had spent her teen years living with the Forresters while the Second World War raged in Europe. She'd been a good student and a well-behaved guest . . . until she'd laid eyes on an attractive young soldier named Miguel Belmonte.

Their fairy-tale romance was a forbidden love with a tragic end. Aunt Louisa had not only demanded that Rosa break things off with Miguel, but the end of the war also forced the issue. Despite Miguel's proposal of marriage, Rosa had been too young, and the draw of her parents and the return to London too strong.

After eleven years, Rosa had thought she'd never set eyes on her first love again, and the sight of him had been a rather personal seismic event that had her heart racing and had stolen her breath.

It was the end of an engagement to another man that had brought her back, a race from the altar and Rosa's stunned groom, Lord Winston Eveleigh. Time spent with her American relatives had brought the emotional healing she'd hoped for. Instead of returning to her job as a Woman Police Constable in London, Rosa had opened her own private investigative office in Santa Bonita.

The fact that Miguel Belmonte had returned to Santa Bonita and was now a detective on the police force had nothing to do with her decision to stay.

At all.

Gloria blasted into Rosa's room, snapping her out of her reverie.

"What do you think?"

Gloria spun in the middle of the room, showing off her dress suit. Made of a shiny, stiff crepe, the slate-blue dress had a tiny waist-belt, a flared skirt, and capped sleeves. Gloria's hair, short and curled around the ears, was capped with a pillbox hat. On her feet, she wore a pair of sensible beige pumps.

Rosa approved. "You look very professional and put-together."

Gloria spun in front of the triple-panel, full-length mirror. "I do, don't I?"

"You do."

"Take that, Mr. Wilson."

The sound of a vehicle motoring up the long drive caught Rosa's attention. "That's Larry. I'll see you at the track, Gloria." She gave her cousin a quick squeeze. "You're going to be brilliant."

Grabbing her hat and her handbag, Rosa took a moment to pat Diego on the head. "Sorry, little boy, but you can't come."

Outside, she was surprised to see a brand-new yellow-and-white Buick Convertible, rather than the old 1948 truck puttering down the long palm-tree-lined driveway. The only thing shinier than the huge chrome grille was the bright grin on the face of Dr. Larry Rayburn, the local assistant medical examiner, a Texas gentleman, and Rosa's current squeeze.

Rosa lowered her cat-eye sunglasses. "Wow, look at you!"

Larry cut the engine and stepped out. "It's not a head-turner like your Corvette, but it's not embar-rassin' like the old Ford."

"I was never embarrassed by your pickup, Larry," Rosa said with a smile.

Larry greeted her with a slow kiss then latched his gaze on hers. "I don't suppose you've got an answer to my question?"

Rosa   swallowed.   Larry   hadn't   proposed

marriage, but rather a move. To Galveston. He had a job offer and wanted her to go with him. She confessed to being tempted. She had seen little of the United States other than California, and she couldn't live with Aunt Louisa for the rest of her life.

She hadn't come to Santa Bonita believing it would be forever.

Besides, there were too many memories in this town, especially with Mig—

"I take it, by your clear hesitation, that the answer is 'not yet'?"

"Not yet," Rosa admitted.

Larry let out a soft sigh of disappointment then opened the passenger door for her. "Hop in, darlin'."

As he climbed into the driver's seat, Larry's upbeat attitude returned. "I just picked 'er up this mornin'." Openly admiring the chrome trim on the dashboard, he added, "It's shinier 'n a button on a preacher's jacket!"

Rosa couldn't help but laugh. She found Larry's southern drawl endearing, that and his boyish enthusiasm, which at the moment was in top form.

Grinning crookedly, he asked, "Are ya ready?"

Rosa adjusted her hat and smiled back. "I'm ready."

2

"*N*ASCAR is the National Association of Stock Car Auto Racing," Larry explained, although the explanation was unnecessary. When Rosa had first heard about the race coming to Santa Bonita, her natural curiosity had kicked in, and she'd spent time in the library and at the bookstore educating herself.

"Yes, I know," she said.

As if he hadn't heard, Larry continued, "'Stock' means the cars are the same as those that come off the factory floor." He patted the dashboard as if he were petting a beloved dog. "Like this one."

"Right," she added. "No real modifications are done to the engines or suspensions in a stock car race, or at the very least, all modifications have to be done with parts readily available to the general public as well."

Larry cast her a glance. "I should know better than to underestimate you."

Rosa rose to the challenge. "The whole thing, including NASCAR, grew out of the illegal alcohol business, what your lot call moonshine. A subset of the economy we didn't have in Britain because the Crown didn't want to give up their nightcap."

Larry chuckled. "Moonshine, hooch, mountain dew, choop. It goes by a few names."

"Excellent marks for creativity."

"NASCAR has moonshine runners to thank. These were a bunch of guys, and some women too, who had spent a good part of their lives drivin' through windy roads in places like the Appalachian Mountains, evading local law enforcement at high speeds."

"So intriguing."

"Imagine bein' dirt-poor, and the only way to provide for your family is to have a job where you have to outwit and outrace the police on dangerous roads with a trunk full of 'white lightnin'." He shook his head in wonder. "These people developed drivin' skills that can't be matched anywhere in the whole dang world."

Rosa wondered how her mother would do at a stock car race. Ginger's driving skills were almost legendary, one might even say infamous, among her friends. That was no doubt also true for some criminals she had brought to justice over the years.

"And some of these men are going to be racing each other today?" Rosa could now see why Larry was so excited.

"Yes, but it's just an exhibition race for charity, the very first race of its kind held around here, I'm told. Car companies like Ford and Chrysler use these races to prove the engineering superiority of their new models. Often the drivers get paid a good sum of money to represent their cars, 'specially if they win. From what I hear, Santa Bonita has attracted some famous drivers already even though it's not as well known as some of the other tracks, like over in Gardena, for example."

After driving through the town and then south on the Coast Highway, they turned west onto a dirt road and followed it another three miles. After a few minutes, they saw billboard signs advertising Santa Bonita Raceway Grand Opening. Upon reaching the raceway, Larry parked the Buick in the large gravel parking lot. The sound of engines revving was audible even as they climbed out of the automobile.

"They're warming up already," Larry said, his eyes glinting with excitement.

The raceway itself was a rather humble construction. A simply built, covered grandstand area seated about five hundred onlookers. Two ticket gates flanked an outbuilding, and just beyond that, was a tall plywood barricade that obscured the view of the actual track. The barricade had been painted white, but there were brightly painted logos depicting everything from auto parts stores to motor oil companies and automobile manufacturers.

After they had picked up their reserved tickets, they arrived at the side of the grandstand and climbed a steel stairway to the upper level. The roar of revving engines filled the air. From where they were, they could see the banked track where eight brightly colored cars, with large numbers and logos painted on them, moved at slow speed in a clockwise direction. The drivers swerved slowly back and forth as they made their way around the track. Rosa guessed this was to warm up the tires.

In the middle of the oval track, a grass field filled with trucks and service vehicles could be seen. A low steel barricade surrounded the outer perimeter. Between the track and the grass were several wide, paved apron lanes where a vehicle could leave the race for mid-race servicing. Gas pumps and racks of spare tires and other automotive equipment were in the pits, along with a dozen men dressed in overalls, waiting.

"Those are the pit crews," Larry said as he pointed. "Each car manufacturer has their own crew. Today, it looks like there are two teams of four cars each: General Motors and Ford."

Rosa felt a twinge of annoyance at Larry's presumption she needed everything explained to her. Perhaps his former girlfriends had been less inclined to absorb trivia.

"Yes," she said. "The papers were quite informative."

In a small wooden tower off to the left of the grandstand were members of the press, both newspaper and radio. A man wearing a suit could be seen at the tower window, preparing to cover the race. A large speaker on the top of the tower promised to deliver his reporting to the watching crowd. Rosa cupped her eyes as she scanned for Gloria and worried her lip when she didn't see her.

Jake Wilson leaned his tall, lanky form against the tower, the glow of a cigarette apparent in his right hand. He was the type who oozed unwarranted self-confidence, always thinking himself the best man for the job, emphasis on *man*. The stories Gloria would recount after a day spent with the reporter made Rosa's blood boil.

Gloria finally came into view, looking out of breath as she smoothed her skirt. Even from this distance, Rosa could see her lift her chin and shoot Mr. Wilson a withering glance.

Another tower—this one open at the top instead of being windowed—had several flags of various colors leaning against the wooden railing. A stout, balding man had his elbows against the rail, intently watching the race cars.

"The start marshal," Larry explained when he noticed Rosa looking at the man. "He controls the race by use of flags."

As people streamed in looking for their seats, Rosa spotted her friend Nancy Klein, Nancy's husband Eddie, and their two older sons and waved them over.

"Howdy," Eddie said. He and his boys had half-eaten hotdogs in hand. Spots of mustard and ketchup dotted each of their shirts.

"Isn't this just the tops?" Nancy said. "So many more people here than I thought there would be."

Rosa retrieved a pair of field glasses from her

purse and brought them to her face. "I'm looking for Clarence."

"Right," Nancy said. "He's driving, isn't he? How exciting!"

"Isn't that him in car number fifty-six?" Larry pointed to a red-and-white 1956 Chevrolet Belair, like the one owned by the Forrester family and, at the moment, sitting in their six-car garage. However, this had several logos and the number fifty-six painted on its roof and driver's door.

"Yes, that's him." Rosa zoomed her binoculars into focus, holding them on Clarence's determined gaze. When he disappeared, she took some time to scan the crowd. She found Aunt Louisa seated in a VIP section with other Santa Bonita elite; Dr. Philpott, Larry's boss, was visible, seated beside his rotund and expressive wife, Shirley.

Rosa's heart skipped as Miguel came into focus. There was a moment after Rosa had first moved back to Santa Bonita when she'd thought fate was at work to bring them back together. Then she'd discovered Miguel had a fiancée. By the time that relationship ended, Rosa had become involved with Larry. No matter what the decade or what was going on in the world, it appeared that Rosa and Miguel were simply star-crossed.

Renewing her acceptance of this undeniable fact, Rosa sighed.

Miguel attended with his sister Carlotta and his police partner, Detective Sanchez. The two were dating, and by the slight scowl on Miguel's face as his gaze landed on the couple, it was clear Miguel hadn't yet warmed to the notion.

Larry bought a full-color, glossy magazine entitled *The California Racer* as one of the vendors passed. He pointed to an article in the magazine called "The Downings: Stock Car Racing's Royal Family."

"Seems we got a royal family just like y'all do in London." He tapped on the page and handed the publication over to Rosa.

The article was about a family from Wilkes County, North Carolina. Two brothers, Tucker and Rufus, were champion stock car racers. Their younger sister Ethel was also an accomplished race car driver, although she was known more for her daredevil exploits such as trick parachute jumping and wing-walking. Along with their father, Frank Downing, the three were former bootleg drivers and had a long business history. The elder Downing had started a highly successful moonshine enterprise back in the days of Prohibition and had served five years in prison before dying in a car accident in 1947, a year before NASCAR had been formed.

As a side and, Rosa thought, an intriguing bit of trivia, Frank Downing's wife, Mabel, had been a circus performer in her younger years and, at age seventy, could still ride a unicycle.

The article explained that the business of illicit liquor was still booming in places like North Carolina, even long after Prohibition had ended. Apparently, there was still a market for booze that was often a fraction of the heavily taxed legal liquor's cost. Thus, the Appalachian Mountains were still rife with hidden distilleries and shady characters.

The article ended with an explanation that the Downing siblings had left any suspicious activities far behind with the tongue-in-cheek statement that they would "never admit" to any specific activities, in the past or present, that were against the law.

Rosa was sure this final sentence was designed to evoke an even greater affection for the family among stock car racing enthusiasts. Intrigue certainly sold tickets. After all, every westerner needed an outlaw to cheer for, especially, Rosa believed, the Americans.

"That's quite a family," Rosa said as she handed the magazine back.

"Part of the reason I wanted to come to this event is that both Tucker and Rufus Downing are in this race. Both are driving for Team Chevrolet."

"Brilliant!" Rosa felt the thrill of anticipation thrum in her chest. The noise of the crowd and the race cars, along with the smell of dirt, petrol, and hotdogs, and American fascination that was surprisingly intoxicating.

"How long are the races?" Nancy asked.

Larry turned to face the Klein family and happily explained. "This track is about a mile oval, and the cars go for one hundred and fifty miles. Some bigger races go as much as five hundred miles and have bigger tracks."

"I hope Clarence knows what he's signed up for," Rosa said, feeling a twinge of concern.

"It's a real test for a car to go flat-out for that long," Larry continued. "For the driver too! Average speeds can be close to a hundred miles per hour." He took a small pair of binoculars out of his shirt pocket and perused the track.

"You'll be happy to know," Larry said, "that earlier this year in Darlington, a Corvette won the stock car convertible race."

"Of course it did," Rosa said with a smile.

"Nobody with any sense could think they could best a car of such fine lines and noble pedigree."

"Haw!" Larry slapped his hand on his thigh and laughed heartily. "I bet none of those drivers down there has ever described their cars as havin' 'noble pedigree.' But the point is well taken, darlin'." He pointed down at the track. "Okay, they're in the pace lap now."

All the cars in the field were now in strict formation at a relatively slow speed as they drew closer to the start marshal. Suddenly, as the man dramatically waved a large green flag, the cars sprang forward as the engines' hums increased to a near-deafening roar.

Impulsively, Rosa cupped her ears with her hands, feeling glad she'd left Diego at home. This was frightfully *loud*.

*a*s the cars thundered around the track, Rosa found she shared Larry's enthusiasm for the sport. Every position change on the track was met with exuberant shouting and pointing from many in the crowd, not the least of whom was Larry Rayburn.

When number fifty-six turned the bend, Rosa cupped both hands around her mouth and shouted, "Go, Clarence!"

Rosa found it impossible not to get caught up in the excitement and was soon yelling and gesturing like the rest of the crowd. Sitting next to Rosa, a middle-aged woman waved a small USA flag. Unable to contain her excitement when her favorite driver had momentarily gained the lead position, she spontaneously reached over and bear-hugged Rosa. Rosa, unaccustomed to such impromptu displays of ebullience, laughed out loud even as she felt her face redden.

For over two hours, the race went on with just two mishaps that caused the start marshal to wave a yellow flag to indicate the drivers must form a single line, use caution, slow down, and not change positions. Several times, Larry leaned over to shout into Rosa's ear and point down at the track. She couldn't make out everything he tried to communicate over the roar of the cars except that it had something to do with 'team strategy' or what number his favorite drivers were.

Tucker Downing and his brother Rufus dominated the race in their respective cars. If they weren't in first and second place, they were in third and fourth, but never for long. On the other hand, Clarence was consistently in the last few cars on the track, sometimes even falling behind the pack completely along with a second car, which Rosa guessed was driven by another amateur driver.

Pit stops were co-ordinated carefully and seemed part of the overall tactics of stock car racing, as well as the use of each other's slipstreams, to gain the advantage. One team member would often block an opposing team's driver when it was clear he was trying to overtake the lead car. Rosa found the event to be thrilling and fascinating and tried to imagine what it would be like to drive in such a race. She would grill her cousin Clarence with questions later.

All at once, a bright-yellow car, numbered forty-four, rammed into another car, causing it to lose control and careen into the outer wooden barricade.

Rosa's heart leaped into her throat. "Wait?" she yelled. "Is that Clarence?"

The crowd had jumped to its feet, and Rosa couldn't see clearly. She pressed her binoculars to her face, desperate to bring her cousin into focus. With an intense sense of relief, she saw that the driver exiting the car wasn't Clarence. The man's face was scrunched in frustration, but he was clearly uninjured.

"It's *not* Clarence," she shouted to whoever could hear her.

Aunt Louisa was on her feet as well, her hand to her chest, but the gentleman beside her appeared able to calm her down. Rosa wouldn't be surprised if this was Clarence's last race, charity event or not!

Finally, the start marshal waved a white flag indicating the last lap, and the crowd was again on its feet. In the lead was a driver for team Ford with

Tucker Downing's blue number twenty-two close behind and Rufus Downing's red-and-white number four in third place. They roared toward the checkered flag, and with a sudden burst of speed, Tucker Downing's front bumper knocked the lead car's rear bumper, forcing it to skid and slow. It was a break for Rufus Downing, who zoomed ahead into the lead.

His presumed win was short-lived. With luck or providence, Tucker Downing blasted past the two cars as the checkered flag waved, edging into first place and pushing his brother Rufus to second place.

The crowd's deafening roar was now even louder than that of the engines as the start marshal continued to wave the finish flag.

"Amazing!" shouted Larry. He then leaned over and surprised Rosa by grabbing her by both shoulders and planting a big kiss on her forehead, knocking her sunglasses askew on her nose, and nearly knocking her hat off her head. He then let out yet another "whoop" and turned back to the race while Rosa adjusted her glasses and hat. She laughed and whooped right along with him. At the same time, she wondered how her posh friends in London would react if they could see her just then.

The winning car turned onto the inner apron and continued around the track—slower now—to take his "winner's lap" while the crowd continued to cheer. The other cars slowed down immediately after crossing the finishing line, leaving the track via the inner apron. Rosa couldn't help but pity Clarence, the last driver to cross the line.

Suddenly, just as Tucker Downing's winning car rounded the last turn, the car swerved abruptly to the right and then to the left as if out of control. Still going at least forty miles per hour, it crashed into the steel barricade on the inside ring of the track, finally coming to a complete stop just below where Rosa and Larry sat. The crowd hushed. The driver's side door opened, and the white-suited driver stumbled out. With blood dripping from his nose and onto his uniform, he took two steps before collapsing face-down on the track.

4

The crowd went silent.

The start marshal frantically waved a red flag signalling all cars remaining on the track to stop and pull over. Members of the pit crews sprinted toward the fallen driver.

"C'mon!" Larry grabbed Rosa's hand, and they quickly raced down the side steps. In a moment, they were at a wooden gate that led directly onto the track. A man in a ball cap and a white T-shirt, with "Santa Bonita Raceway" emblazoned on the front and back, stood guard at the gate, looking stunned and confused.

"I'm a doctor!" Larry shouted as he waved his medical examiner's badge at the man at the gate.

By the time Rosa and Larry reached the fallen

driver, four other men had just arrived. One of the pit crew turned Tucker over and removed his helmet.

"Tucker! What happened? Are you all right?" The man turned to the gathering crowd. "Where's that ambulance?"

As if in response, an ambulance which had been parked somewhere nearby, pulled up, lights flashing. A stocky man in his thirties with the name "Rufus Downing" sewn to his sleeve, ran up, breathing hard. He ripped off his helmet to reveal tousled, sandy-blond hair and wild-looking blue eyes. "Tucker!"

One of the ambulance drivers knelt and immediately checked for a pulse. Larry still had his badge out and showed it to the ambulance drivers. To those pressing in, he commanded, "Please give us some room."

Overhead, Rosa heard a muffled announcement. "People. Please stay off the track. Time to head home." Many curious onlookers lined the fence, but most of the crowd moved toward the parking lot.

Her attention returned to the ambulance attendant, who pressed two fingers on Tucker Downing's neck. After a moment, he gently opened Tucker's mouth, checked for obstructions, then placed his ear close. Gently opening one eyelid, he used a small flashlight to examine the pupil. Even from where

Rosa stood, she could see the dilation in Tucker's eye and the eye's unresponsiveness to the bright light. Larry dramatically ripped open the driver's zippered jacket and pressed his chest.

Rosa's eye was drawn to the pit-crew member who'd been first on the scene. He stood about eight inches taller than Rosa herself and was quite an imposing figure with dark, brooding eyes and a scar on his cheek. A smear of grease crossed his face, so it looked like someone had scrawled an X on his face—one stroke in faded red and one in black.

He caught her eye and approached. "Is he gonna be okay?"

That was a question Rosa couldn't answer. Instead, she asked, "Are you part of his pit crew?"

"Uh-huh."

"I'm Rosa Reed. I'm with the medical examiner. What's your name?"

The man spit over his shoulder before replying. "Rafferty. My friends call me T-Bone."

"Interesting name."

T-Bone's eyes scanned over Rosa's form with new interest. "It's a nickname. From the bootlegging days of my youth. You can blame my crazy pa."

"Let me guess," Rosa said. "You once hit a vehicle from the side."

"You guessed it."

Poor Tucker Downing remained unresponsive to Larry's efforts to resuscitate. The paramedic took over, placing one hand interlocked over the other, and continued compressing the driver's chest at regular intervals. Rosa gave the men credit for not giving up, but she felt less hopeful. If Tucker Downing didn't come to soon, he could suffer permanent brain damage.

"Rosa!"

Rosa turned at the sound of Gloria's voice. Security had created a human barrier, preventing Gloria from reaching her.

"Rosa!"

Rosa stepped toward the men. "It's okay. She's with me."

One of them frowned. "And who are you?"

Rosa motioned toward Larry. "I'm with the doctor."

The man didn't seem to know if Rosa carried enough authority or not but decided it wasn't worth the energy to pursue it. He lifted an arm and let Gloria through.

"Thank you, Rosa!" Gloria said, her cheeks flush with excitement. "It's okay if I take pictures, isn't it?"

It wasn't Rosa's place to say yes or no, but photographic evidence, should it be needed, was always appreciated when push came to shove.

"Take as many snaps as you want," Rosa said.

Gloria had her camera out and was already taking photographs of the scene and everyone around them. "Do you know what happened? Why did he crash after the race was over?"

"I don't know." It was a curious question. Rosa edged in closer to the fallen man, and when her eyes caught Larry's in question, he shook his head.

Oh dear.

The driver's door of Tucker Downing's race car was open. Rosa stepped toward it and glanced inside before walking around to see where the car had hit the guardrail. As she took in the crumpled fender and the skewed right front wheel, she saw a flash of brown, black, and gray slither quickly past her feet from under the car, startling her. About two feet in length, the multicolored snake slipped through the short grass at a frightening speed. In just a few seconds, it had crossed the distance between the barricade where the car had crashed and a group of service trucks parked twenty feet away. It darted under a vehicle and disappeared. Rosa quickly glanced around to see if anyone else had seen it, but everyone was focused on Tucker Downing.

Rosa momentarily stared after the snake while her heartbeat returned to a normal rate. Then she heard the frantic voice of Rufus Downing shouting, "*Nooo!*"

Larry had formally pronounced Tucker Downing dead.

5

Out of habit from her police training, Rosa scanned the faces of the people standing in a circle around the body and mentally noted who hovered there and how they were reacting. Besides Rufus Downing, who continued to express his grief, were the ambulance attendants, and Larry, along with T-Bone Rafferty and three other pit-crew members dressed in white-and-blue overalls. The start marshal was also there, standing next to a stern-looking security officer.

A redheaded, intense-looking man dressed in a driver's uniform stood just a few feet from the pit crew, chewing furiously on a piece of gum. "Carl Ryder" was stitched on his right shoulder. He caught

Rosa's eye for a moment before turning and walking away.

Rufus Downing's muffled sobs reached Rosa, and her heart tightened with empathy. Poor man. To lose his brother, and in such a spectacular way.

Just beyond the circle, Rosa recognized the broad shoulders and confident gait of Miguel Belmonte. His dark brows furrowed over deep-brown eyes as he took in the scene. He nodded his chin in Rosa's direction, acknowledging her presence, but directed his question to Larry.

"What have we got, Dr. Rayburn?"

Larry shook his head. "Tucker Downing didn't make it."

Miguel gestured toward the grandstand. "We saw the crash from where we were sitting. Any evidence of foul play? Or will this be written up as a fluke accident?"

Larry responded with his standard reply. "It's hard to say with certainty 'til after the postmortem."

One of the pit-crew members coaxed Rufus Downing away as Larry pulled a sheet procured from the ambulance over the body's face. During the commotion created with the gurney being loaded into the ambulance, Rosa tapped on Miguel's elbow.

"This is strange, isn't it?"

"Yup. A car crashing after the race is over."

The start marshal hovered, and Miguel waved a hand. "Mr. Stober. A word."

Mr. Stober seemed to recognize Miguel and stepped forward without hesitation. "Yes, Detective?"

"I need a list of the names of everyone involved in this event from drivers to pit crew to sponsors to security."

"Sure thing, Detective. But, if you don't mind my saying, isn't that a little extreme? Tucker suffered a stroke or something. It happens all the time in the races. The heart can only take on so much excitement."

"I'm just cautious," Miguel said.

"Okey-doke." Mr. Stober stepped away and yelled instructions at his crew.

"Where are Detective Sanchez and Carlotta?" Rosa asked.

Miguel scowled at the question, and she felt compelled to qualify it. "I saw the three of you together in the stands."

"Sanchez is on his way. He wanted to arrange to get my sister home first."

Simple and to-the-point responses. Rosa gave up on forced niceties with Miguel and searched for

Gloria. She found her enthusiastic cousin snapping photographs of the ambulance as it drove away.

Gloria spotted Rosa and skipped over. "I got a whole roll of photos."

"Fantastic," Rosa said. She hoped some would be useful to the police because her gut told her that things weren't what they seemed to be.

6

*R*osa loved her office. Rosa Reed Investigations, a second-floor business in the heart of Santa Bonita, had become a refuge from what was often a frantic experience in the Forrester mansion. A small sitting area with a blue teakwood, Danish-style sofa shared space with her desk, which faced the window—flanking that, a bookshelf housing a small library.

Behind a short wall was a kitchenette that included minimal cupboards and a cast-iron bistro table with matching chairs, which complemented the Spanish-tile terra-cotta floor. Rosa had converted a closet into a small but functional darkroom.

Diego had perched himself on the second-story windowsill that overlooked Main Street and the business district of Santa Bonita. If there was one thing that Rosa had learned since she'd adopted Diego, it was that cats loved to watch things . . . especially when they weren't insisting on sitting on the open newspaper.

The moment *The Santa Bonita Morning Star* arrived, and Rosa spread it across her desk, Diego made a beeline for it, plopping his fur-ball body down in the middle of it.

"Diego! Gloria's story is in today's paper. Her first byline! I promised I'd read it and give her my opinion."

Rosa shifted the dead-weight feline—so interesting how cats could be light if they wanted to be lifted or heavy if they did not—and put him on her lap, hopefully, a suitable second-place position.

She picked up the front page, her focus first on a photo of Tucker Downing crossing the finish line, and then on a second picture showing the damaged car. Both images were slightly blurred, but Rosa presumed it had something to do with the quality of the printing machine at the local press.

She read the headline aloud—presuming Diego was, in fact, interested in what was written on the pages. "CRASH WRECKS CHARITY EVENT. Ohhh, catchy. Right, Diego?"

What was hoped would be a smashing success at Santa Bonita's first NASCAR charity race ended in an actual smash when driver Tucker Downing hit the rails after he'd already crossed the finish line. Mr. Downing did not survive the event.

More donations than anticipated were collected in honor of the fallen driver, according to Mrs. Louisa Forrester, who sits on the board of many local charities

The crash is being investigated by the police, who hadn't released any details at the time of this printing. *The Santa Bonita Morning Star* will continue to follow the story: was it a freak accident or foul play?

"I'll have to ring Gloria and tell her I think her piece is stellar."

But before she could make the call, the telephone rang. Diego stared at her with big green, inquisitive eyes as she picked up the phone receiver.

"Reed Investigations, Rosa speaking. How may I help you?"

"Miss Reed, I hope I'm not callin' too early," the gruff voice on the other end said.

"Not at all."

"This is Rufus Downing. Is there somewhere we

can meet? I would like to talk about what happened to my brother yesterday."

Rufus Downing wants to speak to me? Rosa's curiosity was definitely piqued.

"Since you telephoned me at my office, you might as well come here to speak to me as well."

"It's kinda private."

"That's all right. I'm here alone."

After she had said the words, Rosa realized she didn't know Rufus Downing. Letting him know beforehand that she was alone made her uneasy.

"I mean, I'm alone, but next door to the offices of an accounting establishment. Mr. Tindale will know I have a visitor, but that's all."

"Sure, okay. I'll be there in ten minutes."

She had gone to great trouble to make the space comfortable, professional, and hopefully, inspiring. Her small library included history encyclopedias and works on forensic science, which she had read through—some of them more than once. She'd added a library because she wanted her clients to feel they were hiring a well-rounded detective who knew her stuff. Also, because she liked to sit in one of the green-leather chairs and read. Unfortunately, she had had precious little time to do that since opening the office, and it looked like that trend would continue for the fore-seeable future.

Rosa passed the time by plugging the kettle in for tea, then for good measure, she opened the drawer in her desk and stared at the snub-nose .38 revolver. If Mr. Downing proved dangerous, the gun would be a last resort. After closing the drawer, she stepped into the hall, knocked on her neighbor's door, and spoke to Mr. Tindale's secretary, the middle-aged spinster, Miss Weismann.

"'Morning, Miss Reed," Miss Weismann said.

"Good morning. I'm going to Ralphs later, one mustn't run low on tea, and I wondered if you needed anything?"

"That's kind of you, Miss Reed. I wouldn't mind if you picked up a can of condensed milk. We're almost out."

Rosa smiled. She hadn't meant to shop at the grocery store, only wanting to make her presence known in the building, but now, she would have to.

"That's no problem at all. I have a client coming in a few minutes, but I'll go after that."

The whistle was in full force when Rosa returned to her office. Poor Diego had scampered under the couch in the small sitting area inside.

"Sorry, Diego," she said as she rescued the kettle. "That is good and hot now, isn't it?"

Just then the expected knock came. But instead of Rufus Downing, it was a uniformed courier with a package for her.

She thanked the man, signed the delivery receipt, and set the small package on her desk. "It came a day early," she said to Diego, whose curiosity had seemingly overcome his fear. Her cat stared at the package with interest. "Don't worry," Rosa said to him. "I'll let you play with the box."

Rosa opened the box and pulled out a strange-looking green-and-white metal object with the name "Midgetape 44" embossed on the side. Slightly larger than two cigarette packages placed side by side, the device was quite a bit heavier. But it was light enough and small enough to easily put in her carry-all bag beside her camera and her gun.

Rosa had read an advertisement for the mini recording machine in a magazine about office equipment. Although built for use as a dictation machine, she had cleverly figured it would be a valuable tool for a private detective. With the camera, the revolver, and now this discreet recording device, she felt like her technical ensemble was complete.

A second knock came, and Rosa opened the door

to Rufus Downing. No longer in his racing uniform, he was dressed in cuffed denim trousers, a white T-shirt, and a black windbreaker jacket. He reminded Rosa of the tousle-haired, boyishly handsome actor James Dean who had, ironically, died about a year ago in a car accident. The actor had also shared a love for racing and had even driven competitively. Out of curiosity, Rosa had gone with Gloria to see *Rebel Without a Cause* when it was featured at the Santa Bonita Cinema.

"Do come in, Mr. Downing." Rosa motioned to one of the chairs that faced her desk. "Please take a seat." Leaving the door open, she added her excuse. "For the airflow. It gets stuffy in here, even with the window open."

She'd have to keep an eye on Diego—she didn't want him walking down the hall when she wasn't looking, but he seemed happy tucked inside the empty box Rosa had slid under the couch.

Rufus Downing settled his rugged frame into one of the chairs. Now that Rosa was seated directly opposite him, she could see his puffy, red eyes and that he hadn't shaved that morning. It was obvious that he'd gotten little sleep.

"I've just made some tea," Rosa said. "Would you like a cup?"

"I don't drink tea, Miss Reed, but if you have something stronger, I wouldn't say no to that."

"I'm afraid I don't."

"Just as well. Anyways, I'll get right to it. There's something very strange about how my brother died yesterday, but I don't know what it is."

"Have you gone to the police?"

He rubbed his unshaven face with his free hand. "I don't trust the police."

"Why is that? I can tell you that Detective Belmonte and Detective Sanchez are top-notch investigators."

"That may be so, but the Downings have what you might call a natural aversion to the law." His mouth pulled into a slight, sardonic smile, which quickly faded. It was a strange expression since his eyes neglected to join in with the action. "It comes from spending a lot of time evading local authorities on the Dragon's Tail."

Rosa raised her eyebrows.

"It's a stretch of road in the Great Smoky Mountains." Mr. Downing didn't elaborate, but Rosa wrote the name on her notepad, anyway.

"Truth be told, I'd rather be in Hades with my back broke than trust an officer of the law."

"I see." It was all Rosa could think of to say at such an odd admission.

"Where I come from, family always comes first."

"I read an article about your family background," Rosa said.

Rufus Downing cracked a rare, crooked grin. "Yeah, I read some articles about us too. I've never done any jail-time; if you read that I did, it's a lie." Leaning in, he added, "Neither did Tucker...well except for two nights at the jail in Charlotte; the county sheriff had it out for us all there." He scoffed, "Pulled in for a broken taillight." Relaxing back into his seat, he shook his head. "Our daddy, well, that's a bit of a different story. Anyways, we don't need to talk about all that right now. I just want to know if you are willin' to take on this case on behalf of the Downing family. I talked to my sister Ethel on the phone yesterday. She and my mother are waitin' on me to go to North Wilkesboro with my brother's remains. That's where us Downings are from. They are both in favor of me hirin' you on behalf of the family."

Rosa leaned back in her chair. "Hiring me for what exactly? The postmortem hasn't been concluded. It's possible a heart attack killed your brother or some other natural cause."

"It's possible, I s'pose, but Tucker was as healthy as a horse. The family and I suspect somethin' else."

"Oh?"

"The last two races Tucker was in, there were peculiar incidents that happened to his car. A few months ago in Daytona, his front brakes suddenly failed, forcin' him to limp the car off the track and lose the race. The pit crew said it was due to a broken brake line, but they couldn't say how it broke. Then, just a few weeks ago in Raleigh, his engine blew from lack of oil. The pit-crew mechanics swore they'd tightened the drain plug."

"So, you think someone's been sabotaging your brother's car?"

"Yeah." Rufus pulled a package of cigarettes from his pocket. "Do you mind?"

Rosa shook her head as she produced an ashtray. "Why would someone want to do that?"

"Pure rivalry. My brother's been winnin' almost every race for a long time now."

"And you think his death may be some kind of unintended by-product of the latest sabotage attempt?"

"Yes, indeed-ee-oh." He blew out a long stream of smoke for emphasis.

"I am intrigued," Rosa said. "But I'm not a

mechanic. The car needs to be looked at by a professional."

"Already done that with some guys I trust. Didn't find anythin' out of the ordinary besides damage from hitting the guard rail."

"If that's true, then it would be very hard to prove sabotage."

Rufus ran his fingers through his already tousled hair. "Somethin's not right here, Miss Reed. We just want you to do a little diggin'."

"You must have some suspicions. Who do you think might be behind this?"

"On the top of the list? Carl Ryder, another driver." Rufus scowled as he puffed on his cigarette.

Rosa scribbled the name on her notepad. "Why is that?"

"Ryder has a nasty temper. He once jumped Tucker while he was carrying the trophy from the winner's circle to the parking lot."

"How shocking."

"Yeah. Tucker lost that fight and was too embarrassed to go to the police or the papers or anythin'. But he only lost because that coward Ryder came up from behind. The trophy got smashed up too."

"Is there that much animosity between drivers?"

"You'd be surprised at the tempers that flare up

over a NASCAR race. It's as bad as the days of rum runnin' and covert bootleggin' in the backcountry. A lot of these guys have no respect for the police nor their ability to catch anythin', much less a real criminal who deserves to be put in the slammer."

Rosa forced a smile as she stared at her client over the rim of her teacup. "I'm sorry to hear you've had a bad experience with the police. As a former constable, I do hope that one day you will have occasion to change your mind."

7

The Holiday Inn of America was a brand-new, one-story brick-and-stucco hotel just on town's outskirts. Over the front lawn, a distinctive green-and-gold electric billboard flashed. The hotel had a big gold-colored metal star. It was hard to miss when driving by.

Rosa parked her pearly-white Corvette in the large, paved parking lot. If she'd had Gloria with her, she would have asked her to take a picture of her parked directly under the huge green-and-gold advertisement. This very American-looking sign would amuse her parents.

An earlier telephone call to Mr. Ryder had resulted in a lunch invitation at the Lazy Day Restaurant next to the hotel.

Rosa recognized the driver from the race the day before with his easy-to-spot red hair. Wearing a sharp-looking blue suit jacket over a white, collared shirt, Carl Ryder sipped steaming coffee from a white porcelain mug. When he spotted Rosa, he waved her over.

"You must be Miss Reed."

Rosa slid into the booth opposite Mr. Ryder, seamlessly smoothing out her skirt and crinoline slips —a talent severely underrated by the male gender.

"How did you know?"

"I have an eye for pretty ladies," he said with a sly grin. "I saw you yesterday."

Rosa remembered the eye contact they had made. "Yes, well, thank you for meeting me."

"The pleasure's all mine. Do you mind if we order right away? I'm starving, and I got things to do today."

"Not at all."

Mr. Ryder gestured to a waitress wearing a green uniform, a white apron tied around her waist, a white cap on her head, and a pot of coffee in her hand. He ordered a turkey sandwich and French fries. To keep things easy, Rosa ordered the same.

"So, Mr. Ryder," Rosa began. "Are you staying in Santa Bonita for the NASCAR event on Thursday?"

The driver lifted his chin. "I live in the hills, not far from here, but I won't be racing in the exhibition race. Most of those drivers will be either amateurs or pit-crew members behind the wheel. But Chester Freemont, one of the NASCAR officials, asked me to stay, so I am."

"I see." Rosa pulled out her notepad.

"What is it you want to talk about?" Mr. Ryder's forehead wrinkled deeply. "Are you with the newspapers?"

"No, actually, that's my cousin. I'm a private investigator. Rufus Downing asked me to look into his brother's death." She didn't want him to know she was investigating possible sabotage.

Mr. Ryder snorted, a response Rosa expected despite its annoyance factor.

"A lady private investigator? What will they think of next?"

"Possibly a lady who can do whatever she wants." Rosa smiled sweetly. It wouldn't help her cause to alienate her suspect.

The waitress returned with their meals in the nick of time, as Rosa feared she'd either say some-thing she regretted or would bite her tongue off.

Mr. Ryder wasn't kidding when he said he was starving. He wolfed down half his sandwich before he looked at Rosa, ready to continue their conversation.

"If you don't mind me saying, Miss Reed, you don't look old enough for detective work. What kind of experience could you possibly have to do this job?"

Rosa sighed inwardly; it was not the first time she had encountered this response, especially from a man. "I'm sure you'll be surprised to hear that before moving to Santa Bonita this summer, I was a constable with the London Metropolitan Police. Not only that, my mother is a renowned lady detective in London, and my father, a former chief inspector and superintendent at Scotland Yard. You know what that is, don't you?"

Rosa half expected Mr. Ryder to repeat the misconception that he thought Scotland Yard was in Scotland, but he sincerely seemed dumbfounded and at a loss for words.

"You could say I grew up solving mysteries. And since moving to California, I've been called upon by the Santa Bonita Police Department as a consultant, and if I might blow my own trumpet, I've helped solve a few difficult cases. Have I addressed your concerns?"

"Hey, whatever. I'm just here to eat."

Rosa let out a soft, exasperated breath. If you couldn't beat them, join them. She took a bite of her sandwich.

Carl Ryder patted gravy off his chin. "So, what does Rufus think happened that he needed to hire you?"

"He doesn't know. What do you think happened?"

"How should I know?"

"What do you know about the Downing family?" After many, many interviews and tutoring from her mother, Rosa knew that an effective way to begin an interview with a belligerent subject was to ask them for their opinion. Even those inclined to hold back information loved to talk about themselves or the case.

"The whole Downing clan is a piece of work."

"How do you mean?"

"Well, for one thing, the old man was a real pistol. He was always getting in trouble with the law and crowing about it. He died some years ago, but the mother seems intent on claiming bragging rights for her husband *and* her offspring. It's downright annoying. And then there's the sister."

Rosa glanced at her notepad. "Ethel."

"That's right, Ethel."

"I read in an article that she is a stunt artist of some kind."

His signature snort was followed by, "'Of some kind' is the right way to put it. She's a grandstander of the worst kind, just like the rest of 'em. She's been on the racetrack tryin' to prove somethin'. Those Downing boys should get a clue and not let their sister get a foothold in their domain."

Rosa noticed that as his temper stirred, his accent changed subtly from East Coast to something similar to Rufus Downing's.

"Where did you grow up?" Rosa asked. The question seemed to make him pause just for a beat.

"You caught me there, didn't you?" he huffed. "I suppose my Appalachian roots are never far from the surface. I grew up in a small town called Clemmons. I moved to New York ten years ago. But, like a lot of stock car racers, I learned how to drive in the backcountry."

"How far is Clemmons from North Wilkesboro?"

"About an hour. Why do you ask?"

"Just curious. That's where the Downing family is from, isn't it?"

"Uh-huh."

Rosa waited, but he didn't elaborate.

"Have you been back there in the last year?" she asked.

"Sure. My folks still live there. I go back regularly."

"And I am guessing your parents are up on the latest gossip involving the Downing family, specifically Tucker Downing."

"I really don't know what you're talking about." His blue eyes went fierce under his red-blond eyebrows, and his fair skin turned pink. "My parents could care less about what happens to any Downing."

Rosa changed the subject. "Did you ever attack Tucker Downing after a race?"

He scowled, "Who told you that? Oh, let me guess. My 'friend' Rufus Downing."

"Is it true?"

"No. Why would I do that?"

Rosa threw out the bait. "Jealousy?"

He scoffed. "I'm not a child, Miss Reed."

Rosa had only Rufus' word that the attack had happened, so she didn't pursue it any further.

"Rufus Downing suspects that his brother's race cars were tampered with—probably during the last couple of races. Possibly to make him lose or even to cause injury."

"Pwah! That's ridiculous!" He stared at her, his jaw slack. "I was there when he blew his engine. So now you're tellin' me that Rufus Downing thinks someone messed with it?"

Rosa stared without answering.

"Lady, I hate to tell you this, but you're on a wild goose chase if you think that I would sabotage a car over somethin' stupid like jealousy. I mean, why would I be jealous of a cheat?"

"Are you saying that Tucker Downing won the race yesterday by cheating?"

He jabbed his index finger down on the tabletop. "Yes, I am. That race and *every* race those Downings are ever in."

Sounded like a motive to Rosa.

"That's a pretty big accusation, Mr. Ryder," she said. "Do you have proof to back it up?"

Carl Ryder slid out of the booth. "I don't need proof." He pointed at his chest with his thumb. "I just know." He stood, glaring back at her. "If you're going to interview everyone at the race yesterday who has something against the Downings, you're in for quite a long day."

The driver stormed out of the restaurant, leaving

Rosa with the bill. She bit into the second half of his sandwich—no sense letting perfectly good food go to waste.

8

*S*ince she had started stepping out with Larry Rayburn, Rosa had been to the Santa Bonita morgue often, as had Diego, who managed to sleep in his satchel as it bounced against Rosa's hip. The morgue was kept immaculately clean in the hospital's basement, though the faint smell of formaldehyde coming from the refrigerated storage section always reminded her where she was.

Dr. Philpott's office door stood open, and Rosa ducked in to say hello.

"We're going to miss your fine gentleman when he leaves us," the jolly man said with a smile. "But not as much as you?"

The question was buried in a question: was Rosa leaving as well?

Rosa pivoted by saying, "He hasn't gone yet, so we'll have to enjoy him while he's still here. I take it he's in the examination room?"

"Yes. Detective Belmonte is with him."

Rosa felt her eyes twitch. Darn! She didn't want to deal with Miguel again, especially not in the same room as Larry. The peacocking that went on when the three were together was too much to bear. And her own heart—well, she'd just have to buck it up and be the professional she was.

"Thank you, Dr. Philpott. By the way, did you and Mrs. Philpott enjoy the race yesterday? Apart from the crash, of course."

"Oh, yes," Dr. Philpott said, his gaze now busy scanning the papers in front of him. "A veritable hoot."

In the hall, Rosa fortified herself with a deep breath then pushed open the metal door to the morgue's postmortem examination room. Miguel and Larry stood over a cloth-covered body, a small white tag tied to the left foot's big toe.

Miguel and Larry both straightened when they saw Rosa, each taking on a defensive stance: shoulders back, feet apart, arms folding.

"Hello, again," Rosa said to both at once, not allowing her gaze to settle on either. As she lowered her satchel to the floor, she asked, "Do we have a cause of death?"

"Rosa, darlin'?" Larry began. "This is unexpected."

"Rufus Downing has hired me to investigate," she returned graciously. "You don't mind, do you? I've got a few questions to ask."

Miguel knit his eyebrows together. "Why did Rufus hire you? The police are on the case."

"He suspects that someone may have sabotaged his brother's car. And he doesn't trust the police." She turned to Larry. "Do you know if it was natural causes? A heart attack, perhaps? That would solve the matter neatly."

"I'm afraid not," Larry said. "It's a far stranger situation than that."

"Oh?" Rosa raised a brow. "How so?"

"I was just explaining to Detective Belmonte that there was an anaphylactic reaction to what appears to be snake venom caused the death."

"I saw a snake—"

Miguel turned sharply. "You did? Why didn't you say so?"

"I didn't have reason to at the time. But I saw a snake slithering around Tucker Downing's car. I had no way of knowing for sure if it was going in or coming out."

"It had to have been in the car at the same time as Mr. Downing," Larry said. "He was bitten twice."

Larry folded the sheet from the corpse's ankles to expose a set of bite marks on the thigh. He pointed to the left ankle. "There's a second bite here."

"I don't know much about snakes," Miguel said, "but I'm quite sure they wouldn't want to be at a racetrack."

"I concur," Larry returned. "Snakes don't have external ears, but they're extremely sensitive to sound vibrations—especially deep sounds—which shake 'em up somethin' fierce. Any self-respectin' snake wanderin' into the raceway would have high-tailed it out of there as soon as those loud engines started for the warm-ups. I mean, we felt the ground rumble way up in the stands. Didn't we, Rosa?"

The glint in his eye confirmed to Rosa that Larry had made that little comment just to remind Miguel who Rosa had been with. She ignored the bait.

As did Miguel.

"Can you describe the snake?" Miguel asked.

"It was black, gray, and brown," Rosa said. "Very nimble; fast as a whip."

"The poison must have taken effect quickly,

assuming the bite happened at the end of the race," Miguel said. "I mean, it's hard to imagine a driver finishing the race when a snake is attacking him. But is that normal?" He faced Larry. "I didn't think snake-bite victims died that fast,"

"You're right. Not many snakes in the world have venom toxic enough to kill that quickly. I'm no expert, but we have a few dangerous snakes in Texas. Every kid that grows up on a ranch knows something about 'em."

Diego squirmed in the satchel, and Rosa bent low to stroke him. "It seems that if the snake had somehow climbed into the car before all those engines started, it surely would have climbed out the moment they all did."

"Unless he was trapped until the car crashed," Miguel said.

"And if the bite happened after the finish line—" Rosa started.

Larry cut in. "That would mean there were only five to seven minutes between the bite occurring and when he died. Not even a black mamba kills that fast, and the black mamba is in Africa. It's also much larger than what you described. It would be hard to hide a snake that size in the backseat of a car, much less slip it into a car while no one was lookin'."

"Are there tests that can show which species of snake bit him?" Rosa asked

Larry shrugged. "Not really. I'll send a blood sample to the lab, but even then, it's very hard to narrow it down. We can only surmise that it was some kind of poisonous snake and that Tucker Downing had an exceptionally adverse reaction to it."

"What do you mean?" Miguel asked.

"In many cases, if someone has been bit before, say several times, the body can develop an allergic reaction to that particular snake venom."

Miguel rubbed a hand on his chin. "Okay, I've seen enough to consider this death suspicious," Miguel said. "It's possible that someone had it in for Tucker Downing."

Rosa lifted Diego out of the satchel and tucked his furry head under her chin. "And whoever that was," she said, "has a flair for the dramatic."

9

The next morning, Rosa drove slowly down a side street in the industrial section of town. When she found Ricky's Garage on Merriland Street, she parked and walked straight through one of four large, open garage doors into the garage where she saw two hydraulic lifts hoisting two race cars into the air. Each race car had large FORD logos emblazoned on the sides along with black, painted numbers

Dressed in blue, oil-stained overalls, a black man in his fifties sat in an office right beside the first bay, working at a desk. When he noticed her, he waved her in through the open side door.

"What can I do for you, miss?"

"I'm looking for a Mr. Rafferty. He worked with

the pit crew at the NASCAR exhibition. I understand you deal with the maintenance of the race cars,
and I thought maybe he worked here as well."

"That he does, miss. He usually gets here after
his morning workout over yonder." He nodded
toward a building across the street—Stan's Gym.
"You might find him having breakfast at the Waffle
House next to the gym."

He stood up and looked into the garage area,
then pointed a grease-covered finger toward the far
side of the garage. "Looks like he *is* here."

Rosa turned to see the figure of the man she'd
met at the track bent over with his head under the
hood of a stock car. After thanking the black man,
she strolled to the end of the garage.

"Good morning, Mr. Rafferty," Rosa said. The
clip-clopping noise of her heels on the cement floor
announced her approach. "I don't mean to disturb
you. I'm Rosa Reed. We met at the race."

"I'd shake your hand, Miss Reed, but—" He held
out a greasy palm. A toolbox sat on the battery, and
Mr. Rafferty exchanged the screwdriver he'd been
working with for a rag and wiped his hands.

With a gloved hand, Rosa pointed to the top of
the engine. "Carburetor adjustment?"

Mr. Rafferty's eyebrows came together in a look

of puzzlement. "Yes. I'll be racing this beauty on Thursday. It's been a while, but I think I still have some moves."

"I didn't know you raced."

He laughed dryly at that comment. "Miss Reed, you have no idea."

Rosa nodded at the engine compartment. "The adjustment can get a bit tricky on these Fords. It's hard to get a smooth idle setting. One needs to warm up the engine well before turning the adjustment screws."

"And pray tell, Miss Reed. How does one as delicate and pretty as you know so much about dirty engines?"

"My mother," Rosa answered with a note of smugness. "She learned on old jalopies during the war, the First World War, that is. She's a brilliant detective, too. She once told me that understanding engines is a bit like solving crimes. One only needs a bit of patience, a willingness to get one's hands dirty, and something to prod with."

Mr. Rafferty chortled. "Your old lady sounds like a peach. I suppose this pert-near qualifies you to be on the Ford pit crew."

"Quite possibly, but don't worry. I'm not here to apply for a job."

He grunted as he put on his felt Stetson, covering thinning, dark hair.

His red scar seemed even more vivid under the light of the hanging fluorescent garage lamps. Rosa's little joke didn't seem to penetrate whatever good humor the man might have had.

"Where are you staying during your time in Santa Bonita, Mr. Rafferty?"

"Not that it's any of your business, but my brother Philip lives here."

"Is your brother also a mechanic?"

"Nope, and he has nothing to do with racin' or fast cars. He's a rancher, if you can believe that. He's never even been to a race."

Rosa jotted quick notes on her notepad.

"I don't know what a foreign lady is doin' pokin' 'er nose into all this. I already gave my statement to the police b'sides."

Rosa smiled, hoping to defuse the man's defensiveness. "I've been hired to look into the matter a bit closer."

He snorted. "Let me guess. Rufus Downing."

"Yes. Do you have a history with the Downing family?"

"Ha!" His laugh sounded bitter. "That would be a big understatement." He pointed to his scar. "You see this? From a knife fight I had with Frank Downing. 'Twas darn nigh on thirty years ago in the parking lot of Harlan's bar in North Wilkesboro. It was just the beginning of what was to be a long, spite-filled relationship."

"Frank Downing as in Tucker and Rufus's father?"

"Uh-huh."

"He died in a car accident some years ago, didn't he?"

"Good riddance, I say."

"What was the nature of the main disagreements?"

"I don't know what all this has to with what happened at the track, but all right, I'll play along." He leaned against the fender of the car and crossed his muscular arms. "The Downing family hired me quite a few times to modify their delivery cars. Their favorite was the old 1940 Ford Coupe because I could drop a V8 from a Caddy ambulance in those things. It also has a large rear trunk. I think I ended up doing four or five of them for the Downings over the years."

Mr. Rafferty removed a package of cigarettes from his shirt pocket, and after fishing in his trouser pockets for a lighter, lit it up.

"Well." He sent a cloud of blue smoke over his head. "They started being so successful with those cars that I started buyin' into their action, against my better judgment, I might add. As it turns out, they were siphonin' off some of the profits and lying about it to me—I followed them a couple of times when they were unloadin' the shipments for payment and found out. I stopped doing their cars for them, an' they responded by draggin' my name through the dirt."

He removed his Stetson and rubbed his head before adjusting the hat back on his head. "You know what? I just realized that I am tired of talking about that family. Is there anything else nigglin' you, miss?" He looked impatiently at his watch.

"Do you know much about snakes?"

T-Bone Rafferty's expression was one of surprise and then incredulity. Rosa also knew anyone who had lived a life of illegal activities would be well rehearsed in lying to authorities.

"What in the blazes has that got to do with anythin'?"

"A snake bit Tucker Downing," Rosa said. "It's a possible cause of death."

"Well, ain't that somethin'. Doesn't have anythin' to do with me. But—"

"But?" Rosa prompted.

"There are a lot of people who might've wanted Tucker gone."

"Like who?"

As if to make sure no one was listening, he looked quickly around the garage. "I assume you know what racketeering is?"

Rosa nodded.

"Well, the world of stock car racing has its fair share of it, and Tucker Downing was involved in it plenty. So is your current client, Miss Reed."

"Really? In what way?" Rufus Downing had mentioned none of this.

"Let's just say that if you're paid to throw a race by some powerful people, and you go on ahead and win anyways, your ego is goin' to get you in a world of trouble. I imagine it could even get you killed."

"Who are these powerful people?"

"Oh no. I am not going to be the singin' bird on this one. No thanks, I got enough troubles." He held up a hand. "Now, if you'll excuse me..." He grabbed the screwdriver and held it up for her to see. "I've gotta try to fix this idle setting before... as you so rightly mentioned, the engine cools down too much."

eeling guilty about leaving Diego behind in the office, Rosa went back to get him.

"I'm off to the library, Diego, and if you promise to be good and stay in the satchel, you can come along."

The Santa Bonita Library building looked more like a home belonging to someone well-to-do than a state library, especially when compared to the Georgian and Edwardian architecture found in London. A smell of books, old and new, permeated the air, and the hush of whispers and the flipping of pages by quiet readers and inquisitive researchers was like a comforting embrace.

When Rosa had first returned to Santa Bonita,

she could barely muster up the emotional fortitude to step foot in the library, and she blamed Miguel Belmonte for that. They'd first met in this building, and the seed of their short but furious romance had bloomed.

Much to the amusement of those who saw her, Rosa shook her emotional angst off like an 8.0 shiver on the Richter scale. Diego let out a meow in protest.

"Good day, Miss Reed," Miss Cumberbatch said softly. Like many local business owners and clerks, Miss Cumberbatch had fallen in love with Diego as a kitten and turned a blind eye when Rosa brought him along on her excursions.

Miss Cumberbatch had been the librarian for almost two decades and had helped Rosa with her school research projects.

"I heard the race was quite exciting," Miss Cumberbatch said with polite interest. "Were you there?"

"I was. You must've read about the awful crash at the end?"

"Yes, I'm told it was rather frightful. I hope the driver is all right."

"I haven't heard any news," Rosa said. "The papers say it is under investigation."

Miss Cumberbatch raised an eyebrow at her.

"You're in tight with the police. Have you heard anything?"

Rosa wasn't sure what the librarian meant by being "tight with the police," and she could only hope it wasn't a reference to her relationship with Miguel, past or present.

"I'm afraid I can't say."

"Hmm, I somehow thought so." Miss Cumberbatch glanced at Diego's fuzzy head and smiled. "How is Master Diego today?"

Rosa gratefully sat her satchel on the counter. "He's getting heavy."

Miss Cumberbatch ran unpainted and well-trimmed fingernails along Diego's back. "He's getting so big!"

"Yes, he is." Rosa was glad to have matters back in a comfortable arena. "I'm looking for information on snakes."

"We have a lot of reference books on that subject," Miss Cumberbatch said with a tone of authority. "Local or otherwise?"

"Both, I think."

Miss Cumberbatch walked Rosa to the section and waved at the shelves. "Everything we have on snakes and reptiles is here. Let me know if you need anything else."

"I will, Miss Cumberbatch. Thank you."

Rosa soon came upon a thick book entitled *Venomous Snakes of America-2nd Edition* and several more volumes containing snakes in the Western Hemisphere. She found one particularly interesting and spent half an hour reading through a section called "Small but Dangerous."

After checking out a half-dozen books, Rosa could hardly juggle them while holding Diego. It was quite unremarkable when her focus on a slipping book shadowed her situational awareness, and she ran right into Miguel.

"Rosa?"

Rosa's head snapped toward the voice. "Miguel?"

Miguel wore a crisp suit with pleated, cuffed trousers, a long black tie, and a felt fedora on his head. His eyes, nearly always brooding, were dark against his brown skin.

Since her return to Santa Bonita, it seemed that Miguel blew hot and cold. Sometimes pleased to see her and sometimes not.

When he was pleased, lovely dimples formed on either side of a beautiful smile.

There were no dimples now.

"I'm just getting books," Rosa muttered. "Obviously."

"Snakes?"

"Yes."

"Did you leave any for me?"

"I'd be happy to share."

Rosa had started walking, Miguel in step beside her.

Rosa grunted as she shuffled the weight of the books and her enormous cat.

"Let me help you," Miguel said, reaching for Diego. "How is our deputy today, anyway?"

"Heavy."

Miguel heaved the satchel under one arm. "You're not kidding."

"Has the case been marked as a murder?" Rosa asked.

"Delvecchio wants a bit more information. That's why I'm here. But yeah, I think we'll soon be deeming it a homicide."

Miguel ducked his chin, his eyes latching on to hers. "Larry told me he's leaving for Galveston and that you're going with him."

Rosa gasped. Not only had she not committed to Larry, but she also couldn't believe that he would discuss the possibility with Miguel. *Especially with Miguel!*

Rosa spun on her heel and blindly kept walking.

"What does my staying or leaving have to do with you?"

Miguel gripped her elbow, spinning her back to himself. Rosa's heart hammered in her chest, and she couldn't bring herself to look him in the eyes. Instead, she saw they had somehow taken the path to the park behind the library, and suddenly she was in a time, far away, standing in this same park with Miguel who, dressed smartly in his army uniform, had kissed her.

Her fingers went to her mouth as she remembered. It had been her first kiss, and in only the way one's mind could play tricks, it felt like their affair had happened just yesterday.

"Rosa?"

As if being pulled from a dream, Rosa left behind the young girl with her long hair in rolled curls, a knee-length dress, and an armful of schoolbooks, and returned to 1956 where she was a mature lady, worldly-wise, and gun-ready.

She thrust a library book at Miguel and grabbed the satchel, Diego wriggling about inside.

"I have to go," she said breathlessly. "You can have this book. The picture of the snake that I saw is on page four hundred and fifty-six."

Before Miguel could protest, Rosa sprinted from

the park, jumped into her Corvette, and zoomed away.

11

*W*hen Rosa pulled her Corvette in front of her office building, she found Rufus Downing sitting on the step, smoking a cigarette. When he saw her, he jumped to his feet, dropped the butt to the sidewalk, and squished it with the sole of his shoe.

"I was hoping you'd come back. I tried calling but only got your message service."

Rosa carted Diego to the front door. "Have you something new to report, Mr. Downing?"

Rufus Downing held the door open as she went inside and followed her up the stairs.

"Nah, not really. I'm just curious to hear if you found anything new?"

"Let's go inside, shall we?" Rosa fished her office

keys out of her pocket, making a point to yell hello to
Miss Weismann, the accounting secretary next door.
Rosa didn't feel threatened by her client, but it never
hurt to be cautious.

Once inside, Rosa let Diego free, and he did an
energetic lap around the office, zipping over the top
of the couch and desk, scattering some papers, before
stopping at the window and hopping on the sill.

"Well, can you tell me anything?"

"Cup of tea?"

"Do you got coffee?"

"I can make coffee."

"That would be cool."

Rosa went to work in the adjoining kitchenette
and spoke over her shoulder so Rufus could hear her
from his position seated at the little table. "I spoke to
Carl Ryder and T-Bone Rafferty. Both of them had
interesting things to say about your family."

"I bet they did!"

When the coffee had finished percolating, Rosa
poured two cups.

"Cream and sugar?"

He nodded and continued, "I'd give my left
thumb to see Carl Ryder thrown in the slammer."

"He accused you of cheating."

"*What?*" Rufus slammed the table, causing his

coffee to spill over the edge of his mug. "That son of a gun. *He's* the cheater! One time, Tucker saw him pouring syrup into someone's gas tank just before a race."

"That would probably gum up the fuel filter."

He looked at her with raised eyebrows. "That's right. Doesn't damage anythin', but it will stop the engine after a short while. Another time, I saw him lettin' some air out of a tire. What a cheap trick!" He blew air out of his cheeks and spouted, "The nerve of the likes of him calling me a cheater!"

Rosa calmly sipped her coffee.

Rufus struggled to gain his composure then asked, "What are the police saying about my brother's death?"

"Officially, they think Tucker had a freak accident."

"What do you mean *officially*?"

"The postmortem results show the cause of death to be an anaphylactic shock as a result of a venomous snake bite."

"Ana— what?"

"His heart stopped after being bitten by a snake."

"What in the blue blazes was a snake doin' in Tucker's car at a stock car race?" He stilled for a moment, and Rosa could see realization dawn on him. "Someone must have put it there. Couldn't be a freak accident!"

Rosa nodded slowly.

Rufus snorted and threw up his hands. "You see what I mean about the police? It never seems to go our way with them, and now it looks like we can't expect any help from the California version either."

Rosa hesitated before speaking. "I can see their point, Mr. Downing. Using a snake to kill someone is very unusual and not a very dependable means either."

"Somethin' about that doesn't seem right. Besides, you aren't assumin' that." Rufus looked her straight in the eye as he leaned forward.

"I wouldn't have taken your case if I had," Rosa said. "But I don't have a police force to run. I have the luxury of time, *and* if the evidence truly points to accidental death and not homicide, I'll accept that. I hope you will too."

Rufus stared back blankly.

"At the moment though," Rosa continued, "I just don't believe that a snake wandered into that car by sheer blind coincidence."

"Me neither." He shook his head slowly. "But, I am curious to know what it is exactly that makes you believe that?"

"I found something that causes me to think otherwise."

Rufus Downing cocked an eyebrow.

"I visited the library earlier today and looked up the category of 'Venomous snakes in North America.' I found a picture of what I think may be our snake."

"Oh?"

"If I am right—" Rosa retrieved her notebook and flipped a page. "It was a *Sistrurus Miliarius* known for its speed, small size, and venomous bite—otherwise known as a pygmy rattlesnake. They usually bite more than once when they attack."

"Did Tucker get bit more than once?"

"Twice."

"Gol-dang it!" Rufus thrust his hands into the air with exasperation. "What was the snake called? A sis...what?"

"A *Sistrurus Miliarius*. You might know it as a Carolina ground rattlesnake."

An expression of recognition instantly came to Rufus' face. "*That* snake I know about! We call those nasty little things 'mini rattlers.'"

"They're native to parts of Carolina and down through into Florida. But what's *really* interesting is that they are *not* native to California."

Rufus Downing slammed his hand down on the

table. "That proves it! It was not some random snake that wandered into the car. It was put there."

"That's what I think too." Rosa found a dishcloth and soaked up the coffee that had spilled onto the table. "I can tell you that Detective Belmonte is suspicious. He's also studying snakes."

"So, the police might also be investigating it as a homicide, after all?"

"We'll see. But first of all, when would that be likely to have occurred? During one of the pit stops, perhaps?"

"I guess, but they would have all had to have been in on it. It's also entirely possible the snake could have been put there before the race. It just happened to have taken that long for the thing to wake up and get agitated to the point of attacking Tucker."

"That would mean the killer hadn't planned for your brother to be bitten at the end of the race. It could have happened at any moment during the race."

Rufus Downing blew the air out of the side of his mouth.

"Another question," Rosa started, "is why that snake? I mean, there are a lot of rattlesnakes in California too."

"Tucker had a lot of bad luck with snakes. Got bit more than once." He held up three fingers. "The first one when he was just a kid, maybe twelve years old. The second when he was in his late teens, and the third about a year ago. But he never died from any of 'em."

"Why did he get bitten so often?"

"Tucker liked to play in the woods. Not me. I hate creatures unless I can eat 'em. And even then, I want 'em dead first."

"Were his bites all from the same type of snake? This 'mini rattler'?"

Rufus lifted a shoulder. "I am not one hundred percent sure, but I assume so. It *is* the most common type of snake in our particular area of North Carolina."

Rosa gathered their empty cups. She was fortunate that a NASCAR convention would be in Santa Bonita next week to celebrate the new track opening. It kept her suspects in town.

12

*R*osa's stomach let her know it was past lunchtime, so she stopped at her favorite delicatessen and picked up two sandwiches, one each for Gloria and herself. On impulse, she decided to drop in at the newspaper. Perhaps one of the reporters, or Gloria herself, had gotten a "scoop" and learned something new.

The receptionist directed Rosa through a door, which led to a large room filled with the sound of clacking typewriters. Rosa peeked in before entering. Six male reporters sat at different desks, apparently immersed in whatever story or editorial they were working on. Gray plumes from half-smoked cigarettes floated to the ceiling.

Like a lamb on an altar waiting for slaughter,

Rosa saw that poor Gloria had a desk in the middle of the pen. She tapped away at her typewriter but when she noticed heads turning toward the door, followed by demeaning wolf-whistles, she saw Rosa there and smiled. Rosa took that as an invitation to join her cousin at her desk. She'd had plenty of experience ignoring ogling, arrogant men back in London, effectively tuning out their ignorant taunts.

"How are you?" Rosa asked as she sat in an empty chair.

"All right." Gloria lowered her voice. "I have to stay on my toes. I feel like I'm in a pool of piranhas." She nodded toward Jake Wilson, who cradled a telephone receiver in one hand and held a burning cigarette with the other. He winked when he saw them looking.

"And he's the king among them."

"What's he got against you?" Rosa asked.

"I don't have an Adam's apple, for a start."

"Ah, yes. That is why I work for myself."

"I always knew you were smart, Rosa."

Gloria's modest desk had several copies of *The Santa Bonita Morning Star* spread across the top with headlines such as USSR PERFORMS NUCLEAR TEST, and McCARTHY SAYS, DON'T PATRONIZE THE REDS. World headlines such as these came from the Associated Press. Gloria and her crew worked on local and regional interests such as the farmers' market, the latest Hollywood news, and the NASCAR race.

"I brought lunch," Rosa said, "and Diego's waiting in the car. Is there a place we can sit outside to eat?"

"The courtyard in the back has picnic tables."

"Brilliant. You can show me around on our way out."

They were a fortified team as they walked out of the wolves' den. "I don't know how you manage," Rosa said.

"The harassment's nothing new, just a bit more concentrated. The editor, Mr. Mossman's decent though. He has four daughters." She pointed to a closed door. "That's Mossman's office. And the darkroom is back here." Gloria's eyes flashed with unease.

"What's wrong?" Rosa asked.

"Every photograph I took was blurry."

"All of them?"

"Almost all. Jake Wilson laughed like a hyena when he saw them. Mr. Mossman almost didn't give me the byline for the crash story. Fortunately, two were passable. The two in yesterday's paper."

"Which is very exciting, Gloria. Your first published story!"

A smile bloomed on Gloria's face. "Yeah, it's pretty peachy keen."

Gloria led Rosa to an inner courtyard that contained several picnic benches on the lawn. They claimed one and sat down opposite each other.

"So, Rosa, do you have a story tip for me? Everyone has 'someone' in the police or hospital or something. I only have you."

Rosa unwrapped her sandwich. "Well, I was hoping you had news for me."

"Oh, darn! I'm bad at this, Rosa. Was I crazy to think I could take on the world of journalism? I don't know if I can survive a dog-eat-dog situation."

Rosa steadied her gaze on her cousin and felt a twinge of pity. Growing up with money was both liberating and stifling. Having access to virtually anything you wanted could kill the drive needed to succeed. Personal accomplishments, or lack of them, made a person what they were: strong or weak, a giver or a taker, a slacker or a hard worker.

Gloria had already experienced a few failures in her attempts to launch her life so that Rosa worried about what would become of her if she gave up again. A spoiled rich kid with a series of divorces in her near future, most likely.

"Gloria, you must listen to me. You're every bit as intelligent, as strong, and as capable as any of those men you're working with. What you need is determination and perseverance. You can't let others sway you from your dreams and desires. Don't be pushed off your path, especially by an arrogant someone you've only just met."

"Oh, you're right, Rosa. We Forrester women— you, of course, are honorary—are not pushovers."

"You have a lot of your mother in you," Rosa said.

Gloria gaped. "Please don't say that."

"Gloria, Aunt Louisa can be prickly, I won't deny that. But she took over your father's businesses when he died, and they flourished under her leadership. She runs the Forrester mansion like a navy captain on a frigate. Look at all the good she does with her many charities. She's a tough lady, but she's living life her way."

"I hate it when you're right." Gloria unwrapped her sandwich and took a bite.

"And I have something for you," Rosa added with a grin.

"I knew I could count on you! What is it?"

Glancing about the courtyard to ensure no one

could overhear, Rosa spoke softly. "I think the police are going to call Tucker Downing's death a homicide."

"No! Why?"

"I can't relay the specifics, but the nature of Mr. Downing's death proves it. I'll let you know as soon as I hear, hopefully before any of the other reporters catch wind of it."

Gloria leaned in. "What was the cause of death?"

Rosa hedged. "I'm not really at liberty to say."

"Rosa! I won't print it yet, so you can tell me."

Rosa bit her lip before relenting. She whispered, "Snakebite."

Gloria's eyes grew round. "*This* is going to be a *great* story!"

13

*E*ven though five adults lived in the Forrester mansion, as the home was quite large, it was easy to have everyone in the house without them bumping into each other. If it wasn't for the occasional maid who Aunt Louisa had trained to remain quiet and out of sight, Rosa would be forgiven if, occasionally, she thought she lived in the place all alone. Hearing the radio playing the top forty song hits from Clarence's room at the end of the hall brought her comfort, and she popped in to say hello.

"Hiya," she said.

Clarence, who was smoking a cigarette as he sat in a reading chair, looked perplexed. "Rosa? What do you want?"

"I heard the radio. How are you doing?"

"You mean, after my most recent humiliation?"

Rosa stepped inside the room decorated with a masculine flare—dark-green paint and wallpaper, alongside darkly stained wood furnishings. "Are you talking about the race?"

Clarence tapped ash into a tray. "You were there. I came in last. *Last.*"

"You were an amateur racing with professionals. You didn't expect to win, did you?"

"I didn't expect to lose."

"Someone had to come in last, and it was only by a few seconds. The fact that you participated in the race at all is rather something to crow about, I should think."

"Clearly, you've never been last at anything."

Rosa slipped into a chair that matched the one Clarence sat in. "That's not true."

"What have you been last at?"

Rosa cupped her chin with her hand. "Well, I was last in my family to be born."

"Ha ha. Not within your control or choosing."

"I was in a riding competition, and my horse and I placed last." The poor steed had pulled a muscle, but Rosa didn't bother mentioning that.

"How old were you?"

"Ten."

"True humiliation doesn't count if you haven't hit puberty." Clarence's lips twitched with a hint of amusement.

"All the years encompassing puberty are rather humiliating, wouldn't you say?"

"Truer words have never been said." Clarence smirked. "Did you see what happened near the end of the race? The move that Tucker did to give Rufus the win? Being at the back of the pack, I had a clear view."

"Yes, I did see that."

"That's cheating!" Clarence snorted. "I felt like clocking Rufus Downing afterward, and if it weren't for the crash—"

"Is it cheating to help another win?" Rosa pushed a wayward curl behind her ear. "I'm not familiar enough with the rules of stock car racing to say, but you have to admit, it takes a lot of skill to pull off something like that."

Clarence sighed. "Ya, I guess. I know I'm being a child. A man died, and I'm sulking over placing last. Do you have time to share a drink?"

"I'm supposed to meet Larry—" she started, but at Clarence's despondent look, added, "but I'll have a quick one."

They walked together to the living room, where a cabinet was kept stocked with alcohol. Clarence poured Rosa a sherry and took two fingers of neat whiskey for himself.

They settled on either end of a blue low-backed couch, nicely contrasting the yellow area rug topped with a glass coffee table.

"When does Julie get back," Rosa asked. "She's a wonderful little girl and I think you're a good father."

Clarence's expression softened. "Gosh, thanks, Rosa, I appreciate that."

"I know it can't be easy."

"It's not ideal. I wish things with Vanessa were different, but—" Clarence lifted his glass to his lips, letting the sentence hang.

Rosa decided it was time to change the subject.

"Clarence, did you have a chance to talk to any of the drivers before the race?"

He crossed his legs at the knees and sipped his drink. "And here I thought we'd moved on from the race."

"I do apologize; it's just that I've been asked to look further into the crash, and I thought perhaps you might've witnessed something helpful."

He raised a brow. "Someone hired you in a professional capacity?"

Rosa held in her annoyance. It seemed no one in her family, other than Gloria, was prepared to take her work as a private investigator seriously. "Yes."

"But why? Wasn't it just a freak accident? Mom thinks Downing had a stroke or such."

"It's too early to say for sure. Larry hasn't finished the postmortem yet."

Clarence inhaled as he shrugged both shoulders. "I can't think of anything unusual, but I was pretty nervous. All the drivers were focused on making sure their cars were ready and getting suited up."

"That's fine," Rosa said.

"But," Clarence said, "now that I think about it, I did see the Downing brothers having a spat."

"They argued?" Rosa clarified. "What about?"

"I couldn't hear over the noise of the engines being tested, but Tucker Downing flipped his lid and pushed Rufus in the shoulder. The next thing, Tucker was eating a knuckle sandwich. I thought I might have to jump in and break them up, but they stormed apart."

Rosa considered the implications of this new piece of information as she sipped her sherry. If Tucker had been a bully to Rufus, it could be motive, but then why would he hire her to investigate?

"—the dance?"

Rosa shot a look at Clarence. "Sorry?"

"Are you going to the dance at the Town Hall tomorrow night? Gloria won't shut her trap about it."

Rosa flushed. "Dance? Oh dear. I almost forgot! Yes. I've promised Larry." Rosa's brow buckled. "Are you going?"

He scoffed. "Who'd I go with?" Since Clarence's divorce, he hadn't dated seriously.

"You don't need a date to go."

He shrugged. "I dunno. After my dismal performance at the race, I don't think I can face the scrutiny."

"Oh, you must come!" Rosa said, her voice rising. "It's the best way to jump back into the public eye. The band will be so loud, you won't be able to hear what anyone is saying, and they'll just grow hoarse in the effort."

Clarence laughed outright. "Rosa, you're the coolest." Scrunching his nose, he continued, "Ya know, you're right. I'm not going to lag about like a limp noodle. I'll go, but you have to promise me a dance."

Rosa smiled. "Deal."

Grandma Sally entered just as Rosa was about to leave.

"I'm going to watch *The Honeymooners*," she

said. "You're welcome to watch with me."

"I'm meeting Larry for dinner," Rosa replied. "Perhaps another time."

"I'll watch with you, Grandma," Clarence said.

Sally Hartigan took Rosa's spot on the couch.

Happy to see the two enjoying a laugh, Rosa skipped back upstairs to her bedroom. After quickly dressing in a yellow pencil dress with gaping hip pockets, she added a narrow white-patent-leather belt and stepped into matching shoes. With that, she fastened her choker pearls around her neck, clipped pearl earrings to her ears, then pinned a white cap hat on at an angle to her short dark hair. Finishing with white gloves and a boxy white purse, she said goodbye to Diego, who, unperturbed by Rosa as she rushed about the bedroom, calmly groomed himself while nestled in the middle of her bed.

ROSA MET Larry at a restaurant called The Long Horn, and at Larry's suggestion, they both ordered smoked beef brisket with potatoes and black-eyed peas.

"I grew up on beef brisket," Larry said. "Smoked, barbecued, roasted; it don't matter much just as long as the right spices are used."

"I am looking forward to it," Rosa remarked, and she meant it. She was dismayed at the sound of her stomach growling as Larry described the meal.

"Well, first off, I have some news from the office," Larry said after they had taken their first sip of wine.

"Oh? Something to do with the case?"

"I spoke with Chief Delvecchio and gave him my report on Tucker Downing's postmortem. That, together with some research, Detective Belmonte dug up on a particular snake, has convinced the police chief. He's agreed to change the classification of Downing's death from accident to homicide."

"Very good." Rosa expected such, but it was nice to have it made official. She would need to let Gloria know as soon as she got home. "So, Miguel agrees it was the pygmy rattlesnake that I saw?"

Larry looked astonished. "That's right. *Sistrurus Miliarius*. How did you know?"

"I'm the one who gave Miguel the reference book and identified the snake from the article."

Larry snapped his finger. "Of course. I was kinda wonderin' how he put that all together."

"Rufus Downing told me his brother had been bitten numerous times in the past."

"That would do it. Each time, his reaction would

have gotten progressively worse—he was developin' a reaction to that particular snake venom."

Rosa took a sip of wine. "The killer would have had to know about Tucker Downing's previous experience with snake attacks. Even so, it would have been a gamble, because there was always the chance Mr. Downing could have survived one more snake attack."

"Odd in every way."

After the waitress had delivered their food, Larry reached for Rosa's hand. "I reckon we make a good team, you and me, Rosa."

"Yes, I *reckon* we do." Rosa smiled. "But I need to ask you something."

"What's that, darlin'?"

"Why did you tell Detective Belmonte that I was going to Galveston with you?"

That took Larry by surprise, but he recovered quickly. "It came out wrong, is all. I meant to say that you were only considerin' it, and I just...I kind o' spoke with my heart and not my mind."

Rosa suspected that he also had spoken it as a jab at Miguel. She was unsure about how to respond.

"Can you forgive me?" Larry said. He then leaned forward and looked deeply into her eyes.

"Yes."

He let out a breath, his eyes flashing with relief. "That's good 'cause I need to ask the question with the most serious of intention without havin' anything between us that would sway your answer."

Uh-oh. Rosa's heart missed a beat. She didn't feel ready for what she thought might come next. She stared at his mouth, willing the words not to come out.

"I need to know. Rosa, will you—"

Please, don't propose marriage!

"Will you or will you not come to Galveston with me?"

Rosa blinked, her heart stammering in her chest. When the question she feared hadn't been posed, she'd felt relieved, and then, what?

Disappointment?

Irritation?

She held in the sigh building in her chest and picked up her fork.

"I need a little more time."

"Of course," Larry said with forced lightness. "Just remember, I'm leaving in two weeks."

"I certainly haven't forgotten that."

Larry's offer to move with him to Galveston was constantly rumbling in the back of Rosa's mind. There were good reasons for her to go. She wanted to travel—see more of America. It was probably time for her to branch out on her own and get out from under Aunt Louisa's and Grandma Sally's watchful eyes. Texas was a couple of time zones closer to London, which, in an illogical way, would make her feel closer to her parents.

And, perhaps most of all, it would take her out of Miguel Belmonte's orbit. He was the biggest hurdle and enigma. He used to be friendly and happy to see her, but lately, he offered her only scowls and a cold shoulder.

As serendipity would have it, the tension between them was broken by the entrance of Carl Ryder, apparently dining alone.

"Oh," Rosa said to Larry. "That's Carl Ryder."

Larry's eyes briefly flashed with recognition, and then, with his natural Texan joviality, he lifted a hand. "Mr. Ryder!"

Rosa was dismayed that Larry had signaled him. Her last meeting with the man had been anything but pleasant.

Carl Ryder took a second take before recognition dropped. He stepped toward them.

"Howdy, Miss Reed."

"Mr. Ryder. You remember Dr. Rayburn?"

"Yes, indeedy. From Downing's crash."

"That's right," Larry said. "Are you dining alone? We'd be pleased to have you join us."

"That's mighty friendly of you, Doctor. I'd be happy to join you, so long as I'm not interrupting somethin' romantic?"

"It's quite all right," Rosa said. "The brisket is wonderful."

Mr. Ryder placed his order, and once his beer was delivered, Rosa asked him, "How much do you know about snakes, Mr. Ryder?"

The lines on Mr. Ryder's forehead deepened. "Now, that's a peculiar question. You seem to have a knack for that kind of thing."

"Well," Larry started. "I completed the post-mortem today. Your fellow driver died of an anaphylactic reaction as a result of two snake bites."

Carl Ryder whistled as he looked around the room. "You mean to tell me that someone planted a snake in the car? To kill Downing? Who in their right mind would do that?"

Ignoring the question, Rosa said, "How much you do know about pygmy rattlesnakes or mini rattlers? I believe that is what they would be called around Clemmons. Isn't that right?"

"I know as much as the next guy. Stay the heck away from them."

"Did you know that Tucker Downing had an allergy to the venom of the pygmy rattlesnake?"

"Pfft. No, I did not. Why would I even care? Oh." He leaned back in his chair. "I get it. You think I put that snake in the car, knowing he had some kind of allergy to it."

Rosa changed tracks. "Who do you think would want to harm Tucker Downing?"

Before Carl Ryder could answer, his meal arrived, and he dug in with much aplomb.

Rosa shared a look with Larry, and they both continued eating their meals.

Carl Ryder lowered his fork and took a long swig of his beer. He eyed Rosa and Larry then said, "I told you, Miss Reed. There's a long list of names of people who could have a beef against the Downings. But...if I'm going to play along, the first name that comes to mind is Chester Freemont."

Rosa stared back over her glass of wine. "The NASCAR official? Why would he want Tucker Downing dead?"

Carl Ryder threw a bunch of bills on the table then stood. "Maybe you should ask him about it, Miss Reed." He tipped his hat. "It's been a pleasure."

Rosa dipped her chin. At least this time, he had paid for his meal.

14

*T*he next morning, Rosa regretted her reluctance to share what she knew with Gloria. Her cousin, at the kitchen table with a half glass of orange juice, a plate of toast crumbs, and a scowl, pointed with a long fingernail at the newspaper in front of her.

"Did you know about this?" she asked Rosa accusingly.

"Know what?" The question was innocent, but she understood Gloria's anger when she caught a glance at the headline. CRASH CAUSED BY SNAKEBITE. It was an article written by someone named Jake Wilson.

Oh dear, thought Rosa, *someone beat me to the punch*. When she'd gotten home after her dinner with Larry and Carl Ryder, Gloria was nowhere to be seen. Perhaps she should've left a note, but she honestly believed she'd see her cousin before nightfall.

Gloria was unrelenting. "When you came to see me at the *Daily* yesterday, you told me I couldn't print anything yet and that the police had not decided that it was a homicide. I don't think Jake Wilson knew it at that time, yet here it is, a story with his byline!"

"Gloria, love, I hadn't been given clearance to share it. The police had yet to file the report."

"I don't care. It's a dog-eat-dog world out there. Jake has a fella on the inside. If I'm going to survive this, I need someone on the inside. You're my *fella* on the inside!"

Señora Gomez, the family's longtime house-keeper, stood rigidly by the refrigerator. Her glossy black hair threaded with gray was pinned in a neat bun at the back of her neck, and her soft curves were evident under her uniform. With warm dark eyes and a ready smile, the poor woman didn't know if she should keep on with her duties or step out of the kitchen to let the cousins duke it out. Rosa offered an apologetic smile.

"It's all right, Señora Gomez. Don't mind us."

Rosa poured two cups of tea and handed one to Gloria. "Here you go. Tea will help you calm your nerves.

"My nerves don't need calming! I'm not bloody British!"

Rosa couldn't help but burst out in laughter. "You certainly sounded like you were just now."

Gloria couldn't resist the contagiousness of laughter. Her red lips pulled up against her will. "Rosa! I'm serious. I'm already at a massive disadvantage, being young and a woman. Can't you give me a bit of support?"

"You've got all my support; you know that."

"Do I? Will you be my *insider*?"

Rosa considered Gloria's request. She wasn't wrong about being at a disadvantage, and it was obvious by how quickly Mr. Wilson had gotten the story that he'd had an inside scoop.

"Yes," she said after a sip of tea. "Providing I'm not compromising a case by doing so."

Gloria sprang out of her chair to hug Rosa, nearly spilling both their teas.

"Easy there," Rosa said. "Your job is still yours to do and just as difficult."

"I know, but at least I'm not alone amid the wolves. You're my ace in the hole." She winked.

"And, you never know, with my journalistic capabilities, I may be the one to help you on occasion."

Rosa chuckled. "I do hope so. I rather dislike feeling like I'm alone in my work as well."

Aunt Louisa and Grandma Sally sauntered in.

After a round of morning greetings, Aunt Louisa asked, "Where's Clarence?"

"He's pouting," Gloria said, rather uncharitably. "Coming last in the race hurt his pride."

"I wondered what had happened to him after the race," Rosa said. "In all the commotion, I didn't get a chance to see where he went after Tucker Downing's car crashed."

"He left soon after that," Aunt Louisa said. "He was irate because he was came last in the race, and I think maybe a bit shaken up, too, though he would never admit that. I'm just glad he wasn't hurt."

"It is a shame he didn't do better," Grandma Sally said. "The boy needs to feel like he's succeeding at something. Too many hard knocks and a fellow might not get back on his feet."

Aunt Louisa shook her head. "You can't be serious, Mother. Clarence hasn't had a hard day of work in his life."

"And that's precisely the problem. You coddle

him. Why don't you give him some real respon-
sibility?"

Aunt Louisa's mouth dropped open, then shut.
"Señora Gomez," she said instead, "I'll have my eggs
scrambled with two pieces of bacon."

It was an unnecessary request as that was what
Rosa's aunt always had, and the housekeeper brought
it to the table a moment later.

Once all the eggs, buttered toast, and coffee were
served, Aunt Louisa turned to Gloria. "Are you still
enjoying the newspaper work?"

"I love it!" Gloria declared.

Rosa shot a look of confusion in response, and
Gloria defended herself.

"I don't love that Jake Wilson got a byline that
should've been mine, or that the men in the business
go out of their way to belittle and treat me like
nothing more than a pretty face and a showpiece, but
I do like the work. It's challenging and stimulating,
and certainly not boring."

Rosa thought that perhaps Gloria had finally
found her calling, and all that bemoaning not having
a purpose was happily at an end.

"I don't understand why girls these days are so
eager to be in the workforce, only to quit it when
they get married," Grandma Sally said. "Why not

just search for a suitable young man and be done with it." Her gaze darted between Rosa and Gloria. "It's not like either of you needs the money."

"It's not about money, Grandma Sally," Rosa said. "It's about purpose. And independence. About expanding one's horizon and worldview. A lady, even in modern times, must be careful not to develop tunnel vision, only seeing her own small world."

Grandma Sally sniffed. "Having and caring for a family is no small thing."

"Of course not," Rosa agreed. "It's just not the *only* thing."

"You are so right!" Gloria said. "I must get out of California more. Besides our trip to London, I've barely been anywhere."

The mention of London took Rosa's mind back in time. Rosa's American family had attended her nuptials where she was to marry Lord Winston Eveleigh, a marriage that obviously hadn't happened. To Rosa's shame, she hadn't realized that such a union would be a terrible mistake until she'd gotten to the altar.

She and Winston had become a couple on the heels of the tragic death—the unsolved murder—of Winston's younger sister Vivien, who'd been Rosa's dearest childhood friend. They'd mistaken their shared grief for something romantic, at least Rosa had.

To Winston's credit, he appeared to have forgiven her, something she would've said was against his character. As an early heir to his father's earldom, he was rather pompous and self-entitled.

Shortly after she had left the altar, she'd written to Winston explaining everything. He'd replied several times since, begging her to come home, but she had answered none of those letters, and the last few she hadn't even opened. If she were to be honest, she'd admit he was the reason she hadn't returned to London.

No, if she were honest, he wasn't the only reason she hadn't gone back. Rosa couldn't keep Miguel's handsome face from intruding into her thoughts.

"Rosa?"

Gloria's voice pulled her out of her reverie. "Hmm?"

"I asked if you were still planning to go to Galveston?"

"You're going to Galveston?" Aunt Louisa said. "For business? Pleasure? You must let me know if you plan to travel. I know you're a modern young woman, but it's still unwise for a lady to travel alone."

Gloria giggled. "She wouldn't be alone. She'd be with Larry Rayburn."

Rosa shot darts at her cousin. Gloria had the decency to cover her mouth with her fingertips and blink back with a look of remorse.

Aunt Louisa slowly placed her coffee mug on the table. "You're going on vacation with Dr. Rayburn? Isn't that a little...Hollywood?"

"Not a vacation per se." Rosa swallowed. "He's asked me to move there."

Grandma Sally choked on her juice. "To live with him? *Unmarried*?"

"No," Rosa returned. At least she didn't think so. Their living arrangements hadn't come up. Had Larry meant to bypass marriage? Did Rosa give off the impression she would do so?

"A doctor is a very good match," Aunt Louisa said. "But the timing—"

Rosa interrupted. "I haven't decided if I'm going or not."

"Consider your reputation." Aunt Louisa reached over to pat Rosa's arm. "At the very least, let us plan a wedding before you go."

"When are you going?" Grandma Sally asked

"Larry has a new job starting in December. He wants to leave at the end of the month."

"The end of the month?" Aunt Louisa's nostrils flared. "That's less than two weeks away. A wedding arranged that quickly would only mean one thing."

"I'm not—"

"Of course, you aren't dear," Grandma Sally said. "But it would appear to *others* to be the case. No. This will never do."

Aunt Louisa stared at Rosa. "Has he even asked for your hand in marriage?"

Desperate to extract herself from this horrid breakfast conversation, Rosa decided to kill Gloria after the meal.

"Rosa?" Aunt Louisa prompted.

"Well—" Then, miraculously, the telephone rang, and Rosa was, as the adage said, saved by the bell, and doubly so when Señora Gomez announced that the call was for her.

All she heard was "a gentleman" when she sprang out of her chair to race to the telephone room.

"Hello," she said breathlessly. She expected Larry or even Miguel, but when the male voice said her name with that familiar English lilt, her heart froze.

"Rosa?" he came again. "Are you there? The reception is terrible. Do tell me you're all right? Will you come home to me, love? I can't stand being away from you. Have you been getting my letters? I've written so frightfully many. Do I have the correct address? Obviously, you're still with your relatives, or you wouldn't have come to the phone, but seriously, Rosa, these antics of yours have grown stale. Grow up. Come back to London. Yes, much damage has been done, but it can be rectified. I've found a church in Scotland that is simply fabulous, and we can be married by Christmas—"

Rosa slowly pushed the button on the base of the cradle base and ended the call.

If nothing else, Winston Eveleigh was determined.

15

*T*he best remedy to shattered nerves was to throw oneself back into one's work. Both of the Downing brothers had been staying at the Ocean Way Hotel on the Coast Highway going south, and Rosa thought this was as good a time as any to check in on her client. She decided to go to the hotel on the off chance he was in a nearby restaurant having breakfast or out for a stroll.

Once Rosa arrived at the hotel, the desk clerk confirmed that Rufus Downing was not in his room and that his rental car wasn't in his usual parking stall. And no, she didn't know where he normally ate breakfast.

When Rosa turned to leave, a stocky fellow, a

man she recognized as the start marshal from the race, approached her.

"Miss Reed, isn't it?" He held out a hand with a friendly smile. "Rick Stober."

"Yes," Rosa returned, accepting his handshake. "And you're the start marshal."

Rosa couldn't help but feel the thrill of serendipity. The start marshal was on her list of possible suspects. "How are you, Mr. Stober?"

"Oh, still a little shaken up, I would say. What a terrible thing, terrible." He took off his glasses and cleaned them with a handkerchief he'd pulled out of his pocket.

"Quite terrible, I agree. Are you from around here, Mr. Stober?"

"Gardena. That's in the South Bay area of Los Angeles. I can tell from your accent you may not know where Gardena is." He winked at her and then put his glasses back on. "It's home to the largest NASCAR track in the whole region. I've been the start marshal at quite a few big events, yes, ma'am. I sure have, I sure have indeed."

"I'm looking into the matter under the employ of Rufus Downing," Rosa said. "Do you have a moment for a short chat?"

"Oh, yes, of course. Are the police investigating too? Is there something suspicious going on?"

Rosa gestured toward two plush chairs sitting at the far end of the carpeted lobby.

"I will assume you haven't read the morning papers?"

"No. I broke my glasses yesterday and only just picked these up." He adjusted the frames on his nose. "Not quite used to them. So, what did I miss?"

"Mr. Tucker Downing's death has been ruled homicide."

"How so?" He leaned forward on the edge of the chair. "He clearly crashed his car."

"It's what precipitated the accident. Mr. Downing was bitten by a poisonous snake while driving. Twice."

"How unusual."

"Indeed."

Mr. Stober let out an exaggerated sigh. "Any race involving Tucker Downing had the potential for controversy, even at a small track like you have here in Santa Bonita."

"What kind of controversy?"

He ran a hand over his bald head, glanced about furtively, and lowered his voice. "Race fixing, Miss Reed. *Fixing races!*"

"Are you certain about that?" Rosa looked around the room and lowered her voice as she leaned in conspiratorially to encourage him to reveal all, even though there was no one else in the lobby. Even the receptionist had left the counter.

"I've suspected racketeering for quite some time." His voice was just above a whisper. "Illegal gambling, payoffs... You know." As if they were sharing a long-held secret, he cocked an eyebrow. "I think you get what I am talking about."

"Not really," she whispered back. "Please tell."

"Well, there is a certain NASCAR official—"

"Mr. Freemont?"

"I didn't say that." His lips denied it, but the truth flashed behind his eyes. "I don't mean to infer that NASCAR is involved, but the drivers sometimes operate independently."

"In what way?"

"Packing moonshine, Miss Reed."

Rosa stared back, perplexed. "Surely not. Prohibition has been over for decades."

"'Cept now they want to avoid paying the taxman."

"I see. What does tax evasion have to do with NASCAR?"

"Absolutely nothing, I'm sure! But—"

"But?"

"Well, certain races can be fixed, and certain drivers are paid to throw the race. It's another kind of racket. I mean, who could ever prove it? You ease up on the gas pedal, just a bit, and there you go... you've made more money than the grand prize pays. I've suspected this kind of thing for a long time. As a start marshal, you have a bird's-eye view."

"Do you have proof, Mr. Stober?" Rosa asked. "This is a serious charge."

He shrugged a thick shoulder. "All I know is I overheard a conversation in a bar in Gardena just before a race last year."

"What did you hear?"

"It was in the Copa Bar on Manhattan Beach Boulevard. A nice place, really, if you don't mind the cigarette smoke. If you're in there too long, it gets on your clothes. I usually go in there for their steak sandwiches. Their seasoning is delicious. I don't know where they get it or what it's called, but..."

"Mr. Stober, what or whom did you overhear?"

"I overheard Chester Freemont, that's who. He was in the booth on the other side of the dividing wall, talking with two other men. One of them had an accent, like New York or something, and the other sounded normal, like me." He stopped, staring back with bulbous eyes. "Oh, that's not to say you're not normal, Miss Reed. I'm sure you are. No offense."

"None taken. Please continue."

"I couldn't understand everything they said, but I heard some of it. For example, I heard Mr. Freemont say, 'Downing won't do for less than a grand.' And then I heard the guy from New York say, really angry like, 'Last time we paid him a grand, but he still went ahead and won the race.' And then the other guy, the one who sounded—" He cleared his throat and glanced at Rosa. "Like he was from around here said, 'He keeps doing that he's going to make our names mud and cost us a lot of money.' And then Mr. Freemont said, 'That can't keep happening. The problem is that they both dominate the winner's circle, so we can't really go to other drivers.' And then the guy from New York said, 'We may have to do something about that. Maybe we'll teach those Downing brothers a thing or two that they didn't learn on the Dragon's Tail.'"

Mr. Stober slapped a palm over his mouth and pinched his eyes together.

"Are you all right?" Rosa asked.

He opened his eyes and worked his lips. "I've wanted to get that off my chest for months, but I shouldn't have said it. Just once my mouth got to talking, I couldn't stop it. My wife says that I tend to ramble on. That could be true. I know my Uncle Doug loves to ramble. It might be in the genes. But like me, Uncle Doug always means well, I suppose, but it gets him into trouble. Last year at a family gathering he—"

"Mr. Stober," Rosa said, bringing him back to the point for a second time. "Rest assured. I won't reveal my sources unless required by the police."

"What? Oh good. Yeah, I'd be obliged, Miss Reed."

"Is there anything else you can think of that may be of some importance?"

"Well, sometimes race fixing revolves around companies that have vested interests in seeing their products win races. I'm not saying they're all crooked, but it takes a lot of different parts to operate a vehicle. There's everything from oil additives to brake systems... all of those manufacturers want to see their product displayed on the winning cars."

"I see."

"Some race organizers, and even drivers, could have ties to these companies, like in lucrative ways."

"Do you know of any examples?" Rosa asked.

"Oh, no... no. I'm not that knowledgeable about

that stuff." He waved his hand as if flicking away an invisible fly. "These are just rumors I've heard."

"I understand. Is there anything else?"

Mr. Stober hummed as he scratched his chin. "Freemont's originally from Asheville. I know he claims to be from the Los Angeles area, but he's not. A lot of drivers, pit crew, and even NASCAR officials are from North Carolina. Don't know if that helps, but now, if you don't mind, I need to get on with my day."

"Of course. Just one more thing: do you know much about snakes?"

"What an odd question." He scrunched his eyebrows together. "No, nothing at all, I'm afraid."

THE SANTA BONITA Police Station was housed in a small, Spanish mission-style building. Its palm-tree-lined front walkway always looked so welcoming in contrast with what Rosa was used to in London. Though it was November, the day was still warm, and part of her wished that she could just get back into her car and head to the beach for the rest of the day. She would be satisfied with just staring at the gentle surf and watching the seagulls rather than heading into what would probably be an uncomfortable encounter. However, her duty to her client called, and perhaps Miguel had new information that could help her, and vice versa. No one said working with a former romantic partner would be easy, but at least they had maintained professionalism, cooperating for the common good.

"Come on, Diego," Rosa said, lifting her tabby out of the car. "Perhaps you can help lighten the mood a bit." She had slipped him into his harness earlier and now clipped on the leash as she carried him across the street.

The reception officer, a burly black man with a kind face, was used to seeing Rosa with her cat and smiled as he petted Diego on the head. "Detective Belmonte is in his office," he said after a moment. "Go on in."

Rosa walked through the busy open office space where several uniformed police officers sat at their desks, tapping away on typewriters, talking on the phone, or immersing themselves in paperwork. Several waved at Rosa as she walked by, and one officer even grinned at the sight of Diego.

"Your fellow officers," she said softly into the fur on the top of Diego's head. She then realized that perhaps she brought Diego with her subconsciously as a sort of comfort blanket. Diego purred, even as his golden eyes filled with curiosity.

Miguel's office door was closed, so she knocked twice.

"Come in."

Miguel's office was austere and professional with some metal filing cabinets and two wooden chairs opposite a Spartan metal desk near a window with blinds open to let the November sunshine in. A diploma from the police academy bearing Miguel's name hung on the wall. Notably missing was the picture of Charlene Winters, Miguel's former fiancée.

The one light spot was the large birdcage in the corner with a pretty African gray parrot grooming itself on its perch.

"Hello, Homer," Rosa said.

"Hello," the parrot returned. "Look who's here, look who's here!"

"Funny," Rosa remarked, "Did you teach him that?"

"Naw, he just started saying it one time after my sister Carlotta stopped by. Now he says it no matter who comes into the office."

"I hope you don't mind my dropping in."

Miguel leaned back on his chair. Since the age of

sixteen, Rosa had usually been able to read Miguel's feelings as easily as reading a book. He couldn't hide them if he tried. At the moment, she saw surprise mixed with some discomfort. She related to the discomfort part.

"Have a seat."

Normally, the rapport between Rosa and Miguel was witty and fun. It came as easily as breathing and was a chemistry that had been there right from the start. She was not used to being guarded and careful around him.

Diego squirmed out of Rosa's arms and immediately crept low to the floor as if creeping upon his prey.

Miguel watched him over the top of his desk, an almost imperceptible smile on his lips. "I see he has finally made friends with the harness."

"Good thing Homer's in his cage," Rosa returned lightly.

"Good thing for Diego, you mean," Miguel shot back. "Your cat is no match for my bird."

They shared a smile, and the tension broke. Rosa offered a silent thanks to her cat.

"Has anything interesting turned up?" she asked.

"Not really." Miguel tapped his pen on his desk. "Sanchez checked all the airlines flying in and out of

Los Angeles *and* San Francisco that had connections anywhere near Charlotte, North Carolina, and Atlanta, Georgia. None of them reported any passengers traveling with snakes in the last month. In fact, most of them said that would be strictly against policy, even if the snake cage were fully covered and secure. The lady Sanchez talked to at TWA used the phrase 'not on your life.'"

"So, our killer didn't fly here with that snake," Rosa said, "and bringing one by train or even by car would be hard to do without someone noticing it. The killer would have wanted to be secretive about it, not to mention the risk of getting bitten. It's a long trip from North Carolina. It's probably more reasonable to guess that the snake was bought around here somewhere."

"I checked the phone listings for snake dealers in California," Miguel said. "Surprisingly enough, there aren't that many of them."

"Hmm. Yes, one would think there would be one on practically every street corner," Rosa quipped. She couldn't help but breathe a small sigh of relief when she heard another soft chuckle.

"Turns out that snake dealers don't like to keep regular hours. Getting them on the phone is proving difficult."

"I gather a dealer in such commerce wouldn't be likely to have a number listed."

"But perhaps one of the legitimate sellers knows of a black-market snake dealer," Miguel said. "We'll keep trying." He leaned back in his chair and wove his fingers together. "I've been thinking. Have you considered Rufus Downing as a suspect?"

Rosa cocked her head. "Are you suggesting that he hired me to throw me off the scent?"

"It's a possibility we have to consider. He would likely have known about his brother's history with that snake. It's not out of the question that he'd be jealous of this brother. I've checked with NASCAR, and in every race that the Downing brothers were in together, Tucker won the race."

Rosa thought for a moment. "He did tell me he had his own mechanics look at the car."

Miguel pointed his pen at her. "There you go. And I bet he told you they found nothing. Sibling rivalry can be a strong motive for murder. It certainly wouldn't be the first time."

"It wouldn't be the first time a client has hired me, only for me to discover later that my client was complicit."

"Thereby, totally underestimating you," Miguel added with a small grin. "A big mistake."

"Indeed."

They both looked at each other for a long moment.

His office suddenly felt too small.

"What about you, Rosa?" Miguel finally said. "Do you have anything to share with the police?"

Rosa noted how he didn't say "with me," keeping her at arm's length. She didn't blame him. She suffered from complicated emotions when it came to Miguel and surmised that he must feel the same way. Best to say her part and get going.

"I ran into Mr. Stober this morning."

Miguel checked his notes. "The acting start marshal?"

"Yes. I was looking for Rufus Downing at his hotel, so our meeting was a happy accident."

"And—"

"Mr. Stober's a talkative fellow, but eventually, he revealed a conversation he'd overheard involving Mr. Freemont."

Miguel scanned his notes again.

"A NASCAR official."

"Yes. Mr. Stober's quite certain that the topic of conversation was race fixing."

Miguel's dark eyebrows arched, drawing attention to his stunning copper-colored eyes. Rosa found herself captivated momentarily as his dark eyelashes blinked.

"Rosa?"

"Oh, yes, forgive me," Rosa said, recovering. "I was just recalling the conversation. Mr. Stober believes that drivers are sometimes paid to lose deliberately. It's part of a gambling gimmick."

"That would make for an interesting motive. Had Tucker Downing crossed anyone lately?"

"I can only assume. After my chat with Mr. Stober, I waited around hoping that Rufus Downing would show up. I'd like to ask him more questions about this."

"You and me both," Miguel said.

His telephone rang, and he held up a finger indicating that Rosa should wait while he answered it.

Diego, in the meantime, had Homer in his sights but had softened into a relaxed stance. Perhaps one day, the two creatures could be friends and the cage wouldn't be necessary protection, either for Diego or for Homer.

Miguel's expression turned sour as he listened. After hanging up, he locked eyes with Rosa.

"I'm afraid neither of us is going to get to ask Rufus Downing anything. He's dead."

16

*R*osa thought she owed it to Gloria to swing by the newspaper and pick her up. Her cousin's long-lasting look of offense lightened when Rosa whispered her news. "A car found over the embankment by two hikers had Rufus Downing's body in it. He had rented the car."

"Oh?" With a short glance at Jake Wilson, who'd just answered his ringing phone, Gloria quickly gathered her leather satchel, which contained her camera and notebooks. "I'm coming with you."

"Of course," Rosa said. "That's why I'm here."

Rosa knew the winding road. It started just a few miles east of Santa Bonita and headed up the Santa Ynez mountains, gaining about 1800 feet in elevation before coming down the other side. For the last few months, there had been bridge construction just past the summit, closing the road at the top. This meant the only traffic on the road was the odd car heading up to take in the view at a spot where part of the mountain had broken away into a dangerous cliff called Inspiration Lookout. The spot offered an incredible view of the whole town of Santa Bonita and the Pacific, and Gloria had taken Rosa up to it just after she had first arrived from England early in the summer.

"You're sure it's Rufus Downing?" Gloria asked. Wisps of her hair, now neatly tucked under a silk scarf much like Rosa's, blew out under the force of the winds created by the speeding Corvette.

"According to Miguel, the responding officers found identification on the body."

Gloria lowered her sunglasses to stare at Rosa. "According to *Miguel*? I thought you two were on the outs."

Rosa pretended not to hear Gloria and instead rubbed a hand over Diego's head. Her pet nestled in the satchel sitting between them.

The traffic on the road was light, and they made good time, something Gloria delighted in.

"We beat Jake! I just know that was the call I saw

him pick up. He's got someone in the police who feeds him leads."

Rosa parked just behind a row of black-and-white Fords, each with a flashing red bulb on the roof.

"Diego should probably stay," Rosa said as she brought the roof of the convertible to a close. Clearly disapproving the move, Diego jumped out of his satchel, but Rosa knew he'd protest and grabbed his collar before he could scamper off.

Gloria, eager to beat Jake to get the story, hurried ahead of Rosa, who, managing to keep Diego captive in her car, caught up a few minutes later.

As she got closer, Rosa saw a tow truck with Gord's Towing painted on the door. The tow truck had a cable attached to a winch, and two men were carefully descending the steep incline along the edges of the area where the cliff had broken sharply. A blue Ford lay at the bottom of a ravine about fifty feet below. It looked like the car hadn't made the curve, going off the road at the worst possible spot.

Miguel and Detective Sanchez looked over the edge as Rosa and Gloria approached and took in the scene. The front of the car was crumpled around a large tree, and the hood had been driven through the front windshield and into the front seat. It would have killed anyone sitting there.

Gloria had her camera out and snapped pictures. Watching this, Rosa understood why Gloria's photographs were blurry.

"Gloria," she said quietly. "Slow down a bit and steady your camera more. It would help if you took the time to focus the lens and center the frame. Take a breath between your shots."

"Ah," Gloria said. "Thank you."

"Ambulance has already taken the body," Sanchez said as he nodded toward the departing white Caddy. "What was left of it, anyways."

Rosa looked at Miguel questioningly.

"It's pretty clear he died on impact," he answered,

"Two Downing brothers in less than a week," Rosa said.

"Not sure how long ago it happened." Sanchez scratched his head and took a puff on his cigarette. "Probably sometime this morning. It took the hikers a couple of hours to get down the mountain and to a phone booth."

"We'll know more after Dr. Philpott takes a look," Miguel said.

Rosa noticed he didn't say Larry Rayburn even

though he was the one likely to be participating in an autopsy.

"Maybe drunk?" Sanchez offered. "The whole car stank like whiskey."

Miguel stuffed his fists into his khaki pants. "He'd have had to start drinking in the morning, I would say."

Rosa frowned. "I can't imagine a prize-winning racing car driver, someone who learned his skills on some of the most challenging roads in America, would get stone-drunk, lose control of his rental car, and crash down a ravine."

"*Three days* after his brother died," Gloria added.

"He's distraught over losing his brother," offered Detective Sanchez. "He goes on a bit of a binge and loses control."

Rosa gazed down the cliff. "I would be more inclined to say the death was somehow staged."

"That would be a bit of a feat," Sanchez remarked.

"In any event," Miguel said, catching Rosa's eye. "It looks like you just lost your client."

Officer Richardson joined them with his police camera at the ready. He scowled at Rosa and gave Gloria and her camera a withering glance. Rosa thought it best that the two get out of the way of the police.

As Gloria had suspected, Jake Wilson joined the small crowd. Rosa saw the sly smile of triumph Gloria couldn't resist offering to the man who had been doing a poor job of mentoring her.

Once their backs were turned, Gloria said, "Quick, what do you know that he can't find out from the police."

Rosa bristled at the feeling of becoming a pawn in Gloria's game. "I don't know anything that you don't know."

Gloria whined. "I've just got to write a better story than Jake."

"Why?" Rosa countered. "He's the established reporter, and you're an apprentice. It's normal that he would have a certain amount of seniority."

"Yeah, but—"

"And why are you calling him by his first name? You sound like a jilted lover rather than someone bothered by a colleague."

Gloria blushed at Rosa's insinuation. "We are not lovers!"

"Of course not," Rosa said soothingly, but her feminine intuition was on alert. Her cousin's behavior looked like "the lady doth protest too much," and Rosa wondered if Gloria was attracted to the man she insisted she despised.

She sighed softly. Matters of the heart were a complicated affair.

Gloria blew a raspberry. "I suppose we should go."

"I rather think we should wait."

Gloria shifted the strap of her leather satchel over her shoulder. "I have to get back to the newspaper, Rosa."

Her client might be dead, but Rosa had no intention of dropping her investigation. She had banked Rufus Downing's check—an upfront deposit—and owed it to him to do her best to seek justice for both him and his brother.

"Can you get a lift?" Rosa said. She was about to suggest Miguel and Detective Sanchez, but she didn't want them to know she was hanging back.

"I suppose I could ask Jake," Gloria said, then amended, "or should I say, Mr. Wilson."

"That would be terrific."

With some effort, Rufus Downing's rental car was pulled from the ravine by the tow truck along an easier trajectory than the one it had gone down on. It was then towed away from the scene. The police cars followed along with Gloria and Mr. Wilson—neither looking like they hated the other. Rosa feared Gloria's current beau, Ben Applebaum, might be in for a broken heart or at least damaged pride.

Rosa returned to the edge of the road where the car had gone off. It was plain to see the trajectory of the car as it had crashed its way down the cliff. Near the top, the ground was covered in gravel, but further down, it gave way to large rocks before it turned to the tree line. Some of the smaller trees had been bowled over, and a few had some bark torn off, including the one that had stopped the car, killing Rufus Downing.

Rosa wanted her own photographs. Officer Richardson wasn't about to share his findings with her, and who knew if Gloria's film would turn out.

She returned to her Corvette to retrieve her own Argus camera, but just as she strapped it around her neck, Diego, having had enough of being locked up, darted out and along the side of the embankment.

"Diego!"

Rosa ran after her cat, thankful for the ballet flats she wore, but the dratted creature scurried ahead just out of reach. He'd stop, but just as she would be close enough to grab him, he'd dash ahead.

"Diego, you little rascal!"

In for a penny, in for a pound, Diego scooted

down the side of the ravine that, though dotted with prickly thistles, was at a softer incline. He continued to the bottom where the hikers had been walking along the creek and on to the tree line where Rufus Downing's rental car had been stopped.

Rosa thought she had her chance to capture her rebellious feline when he lingered over a beetle bug, but once again, he eluded capture, only this time he chased a squirrel up a pine tree.

"Diego! This isn't funny!"

Diego, sitting primly on a branch about ten feet off the ground, blinked back slowly, his expression looking smug and not at all repentant.

"Fine," Rosa said, pivoting in the opposite direction. "Have your way. The owls will make a meal of you by midnight."

Making fine theater of strolling back to the Corvette, Rosa cast a glance over her shoulder. Diego seemed to have had a change of heart and was trying to get down. However, he'd underestimated how far ten feet was and couldn't find a way to make it down to the next lower branch.

Rosa moaned. "Don't tell me I have to climb up there and get you."

Diego expressed his remorse with a loud meow.

"All right, all right. But don't say I didn't warn you."

Rosa's childhood had given her plenty of opportunities to climb trees. There was a sturdy walnut tree in the back garden of Hartigan House, and the land around Bray Manor, the Gold family's country estate, was particularly inviting for adventurous spirits like Rosa's.

"It's been a while," Rosa said aloud, "but it's like riding a bike." She hoisted herself up one branch at a time, eventually reaching her repentant pet. "You'll have to ride down on my back." Rosa gingerly placed Diego over her shoulders, wincing at his enthusiastic grip. "I'll have to clip your nails when we get back to the Forrester mansion."

Just as she twisted her body to reach for the branch beneath her with her toe, she caught sight of something strange along the face of the cliff, something one could only see from this vantage point.

"Isn't that interesting," Rosa said. Swinging both feet up and around a bottom branch, she shifted her weight upright. To balance herself, she hooked her arm around the trunk, which freed both hands. While Diego meowed loudly, Rosa managed to grip her camera as it dangled from its cord around her neck and snap half a dozen pictures. Diego inched his way along the branch just above and climbed onto her head.

What a team *we* make, Rosa thought as she struggled with both her camera and her cat while trying not to fall out of the tree.

17

*A*fter Mr. Stober's accusation against Chester Freemont about fixed racing, Rosa was determined to question the NASCAR organizer. She suspected he'd be involved with the setting up of things at the Santa Bonita Rotary Hall and found him in the large area supervising two men on stepladders as they hung a massive cloth banner across the top of the stage area. The banner had various logos on it, but the main feature was the huge letters painted in white on a black background: NASCAR.

Wearing a light-blue cardigan sweater over a white, collared shirt, gray slacks, and a black tie, the NASCAR official reminded Rosa of a bird of prey with his angular facial features and long, thin nose.

The room buzzed with activity as people set up display booths representing various car manufacturers, car parts distributors, and subscription magazines, as well as erecting autograph booths. But the centerpiece of the room was a gleaming, green car parked in the middle of a square, chained-off area. One could get close to the car but not close enough to touch it. Painted on the door in stylized white-and-orange lettering were the words "Fabulous Hudson Hornet." The front hood was left open to allow the crowd to study the engine.

As Rosa walked over to the car to look, Chester Freemont caught her eye and joined her. "Say, didn't I see you at the racetrack Sunday?"

"Quite likely." She shook his outstretched hand. "Rosa Reed."

"Chester Freemont." He gestured to the green car. "She's a beauty, isn't she? She's won a lot of races for Hudson Cars. Marshall Teague, Herb Thomas, and a few others have had the pleasure of driving her."

"I'm afraid I am not familiar with those names."

"Marshall Teague is one of the best drivers on the circuit. He's going to be here signing autographs at the convention, if you're planning to attend."

"I just might do that," Rosa said as she glanced

about the place. "Wow, there's a lot of preparation going on. Have you been here all morning?"

Mr. Freemont tucked both thumbs around his belt buckle and rocked on his heels. "Uh-huh. Most of the morning, anyways. I did go for a walk on the beach before I came." He regarded Rosa for a moment. "What brings you here today, Miss Reed? A new fascination with racing? Plenty of young ladies find the sport exciting."

"Actually, I work as a private investigator and have been recently hired by Rufus Downing to look into the death of his brother."

News of her client's death hadn't yet been made public—that was certain to change by the time the evening news hit the airwaves—and she didn't feel it necessary to elaborate. And had Mr. Freemont been involved in Rufus Downing's demise, Rosa didn't want to play her hand.

The man frowned. "Doesn't seem like the job for a pretty little lady such as yourself."

"And yet, here I am, doing the very job."

"Aren't the police in charge? I read in the paper this morning they've decided Tucker's crash wasn't an accident."

"Yes, and though I work independently, I also cooperate with the police." Rosa jumped into her next question. "Have you ever heard of a mini rattler?"

Mr. Freemont tapped his nose with his forefinger. "You mean like a snake?"

"That's what they call it in North Carolina. It's more commonly referred to as a pygmy rattlesnake. It's the snake that bit Tucker Downing during the race on Sunday."

"Is that right? Well, I'm afraid I don't know anything about snakes."

"Have you ever spent much time in North Carolina?"

"No, I've never been there. I'm sure it's nice."

Mr. Stober had been speaking the truth. Mr. Freemont didn't want people to know he was from Asheville.

Rosa waited until Chester Freemont's gaze landed on her. "Mr. Freemont, do you know of anyone who has been involved in race fixing?"

"Race fixing? I don't... I don't..."

Rosa noticed a change in pupil dilation and the rhythm of his breathing.

"Race fixing?" he said again. He shook his head. "I'm on the board of NASCAR, Miss Reed. I'm not involved in that kind of thing, and I wouldn't know anyone who was!"

Rosa knew from experience that people who lie often repeat phrases; it was a subconscious way to buy some time to think of a suitable response.

"So, it doesn't go on at all at NASCAR races?" Rosa pressed.

"Race fixing in NASCAR?" The corner of his eye twitched. "No way, certainly not."

He was lying.

WHOEVER KILLED Tucker Downing must have been aware of his previous contact with pygmy rattlesnakes, a detail not widely known. Rosa surmised that it was most likely someone who had heard about Tucker's reptilian misfortunes through local gossip in North Carolina, or perhaps from a family member. Regardless, Rosa wanted to know why Chester Freemont had lied about never having been there.

A soft chuckle from behind caught her attention, and Rosa turned to see a tall man dressed in a Stetson, flannel shirt, denim trousers, and cowboy boots. In his late forties, he leaned nonchalantly against a post. The man's resemblance to T-Bone Rafferty was uncanny—he even wore the same type of hat. His impressive horseshoe mustache descended on each side of his mouth down to his jawline. Missing was the knife scar on the left cheek.

"Miss Reed, if I'm not mistaken." His voice was not as gravelly as T-Bone's, and he carried no hint of an Appalachian accent.

Rosa smiled. "I'm afraid you have the advantage."

Extending a rough hand, he said, "The name's Philip Rafferty."

"Pleased to meet you."

"My brother is a NASCAR mechanic and, now that I live here—just moved west last spring—he recruited me to help him out. As you can see, this attraction brings in a lot of men. I can't help but notice when a pretty young lady such as yourself walks in."

"That's very kind of you to say, Mr. Rafferty."

"Such a pretty accent, if you don't mind my saying so. England?"

"London."

"Been there once. Too crowded for my liking. Even worse than Los Angeles."

"London is loved by many and hated by many as well," Rosa conceded.

"Well, if you'd like a tour of Santa Bonita, I'd be happy to oblige."

"That's nice to know, but I'm wondering if you'd mind if I asked you a couple of questions."

His blue eyes flashed with bemusement. "Shoot."

"I have to confess, I'm already acquainted with your brother, T-Bone. I'm investigating the recent death of Tucker Downing, at the request of his brother, Rufus Downing."

His brow crumpled. "Huh?"

"I work in Santa Bonita as a private investigator."

Philip Rafferty's gaze scanned Rosa from the top of her hatless head to her ballet flats "You? A private dick."

Deadpan, Rosa responded. "I prefer the term 'gumshoe.'"

He crossed his arms, taking a small step back. "I already talked to the police."

"You were at the race when Tucker Downing crashed?"

"Me and hundreds of other spectators."

"Do you or your brother have anything to do with snakes?"

"Huh? Oh, I heard ol' Tucker got bit by something. What did that have to do with his crash?"

"A snake was put in his car."

"Ah. Well, that's kind of sinister, isn't it?"

"Yes."

"But to answer your question, my brother and I hate snakes."

"Where were you this morning between, say, from seven a.m. until now?"

"Not sure what business it is of yours, but I was on my ranch, fixing a fence."

"Can anyone vouch for that?"

"Doubtful. Why are you asking?"

"Rufus Downing was involved in an automobile accident this morning. The circumstances appear suspicious."

"Ha! That family has the worst luck."

Rosa found his lack of empathy concerning, even if she hadn't revealed Rufus's ultimate demise.

"At least, this time, they didn't kill anyone else."

"What does that mean?" Rosa asked.

"On a stretch of highway the locals call 'The Tail of the Dragon,' not far from the famous Cheoah Dam, two young fellows drove over a cliff trying to avoid an oncoming car driven by Tucker Downing, who was accompanied by Rufus Downing. The police labeled it an accident, and no charges were laid."

"Who were the two men who died?"

"They were my sons." He looked away and rubbed his chin.

"I am so sorry to hear that." A tragic story. Rosa couldn't help but feel sympathy. It also, unfortunately, thrust Philip Rafferty to the top of the suspect list.

The man was smart enough to realize this. He looked at her directly. "I've made my peace with it, Miss Reed. I don't believe those Downing boys had any malicious intent. Why would they? They didn't even know my boys. They were driving recklessly, but no doubt, my boys were too. It's like some badge of honor to drive that windy stretch of highway at high speeds, and I can easily picture my James and Timothy racing around those dangerous curves like their uncle T-Bone used to do. They were driving one of his modified Fords at the time."

He sighed heavily and adjusted his Stetson. "T-Bone and I don't talk about it. It's over and done." He nodded curtly, adding, "And I think this conversation is too." After tipping the brim of his hat, he walked away.

18

*J*ust as Rosa was heading toward the exit doors, she noticed Chester Freemont, with his back to her, standing near one of the display booths. He spoke animatedly in a low voice to a snappily dressed middle-aged man in a black, pin-striped suit. The man reminded Rosa of a professional wrestler with his broad shoulders and large hands and looked rather ostentatious in his expensive suit which he paired with patent-leather shoes and a gray fedora, cocked to one side. His sharp, keen eyes kept glancing around the room while he talked. Rosa quickly picked up a brochure from a nearby display that was advertising Michelin tires and pretended to be engrossed in the new fall line of all-season tread designs.

One of the booths close to where the two men huddled together had a life-sized cutout of a race car driver nicknamed "Rapid Reggie." The booth was obviously being set up for autographs, but at the moment there was no one there. It was a perfect place to eavesdrop without being seen, and Rosa slipped in behind the cutout, where she could just make out snatches of their conversation.

She heard Chester Freemont's voice. "It looks like it went off without a hitch. Nice work, you guys can be proud. The other drivers will no doubt be sure to keep this little lesson in mind before they try to cross us again."

"I am always proud of my work," the other man said. Rosa was surprised to hear a pronounced East Coast accent, and guessed the man was from New York.

He continued, "I'll make sure and pass on your good will. But for now, I'll stick around for a few days."

The rest of the conversation was lost as the two men gradually drifted further away from Rosa's position, and she couldn't follow them without being seen. However, she'd heard enough to suspect that perhaps this was the man that Rick Stober had heard in conversation with Chester Freemont in Gardena.

Rosa watched Chester Freemont's well-dressed companion, as the man split off from the pairing, getting intercepted by a young man dressed in over-alls. The fellow worked his way down a step ladder, having just finished attaching a large sign to the top of one of the more elaborate displays: *Mainline Shocks and Struts.*

After a short conversation, the man tipped his hat, and then, with confidence oozing, strutted over to a beautiful blonde lady, where giggling flirtation ensued.

Rosa approached the workman, held out her hand, smiled and donned a thick American accent.

"Hi there. My name is Beth Kramer and I'm with *The Santa Bonita Morning Star.*" She fluttered her eyelashes and smiled brightly. "You're pretty brave to be up there so high on this thing." Rosa put her hand on the stepladder and made a point of staring at the top of it.

"Oh?" said the man in surprise, "Yeah... I guess so." He smiled back shyly.

"Say, I was hoping to get an interview with that man over there talking to the pretty blonde." She pulled out her notepad and pretended to consult it.

"I have his name here somewhere. Mr...." she scrolled her finger down an imaginary list.

"Talbot... Cy Talbot."

"Right. An important man around here." Rosa chuckled. "I should remember his name. Anyway, I saw you talking to him just now and I thought it might be interesting to get an insider view of what Mr. Talbot does. Would that be okay? I bet you're from out of town, aren't you? Now what's your name?" Rosa smiled flirtatiously and held her pen over her notepad.

The flustered young man seemed to have forgotten his name momentarily. "Uhm... I. Oh... yeah, my name is Pete Johannson. I am with the company."

Rosa glanced up at the sign. "Mainline Shocks and Struts."

"That's right. We're here at all the West Coast races setting up booths and stuff. East Coast too, but I live in Santa Monica so I'm usually the guy doing the West Coast set ups."

"Sounds absolutely fascinating," Rosa said. "And how exactly is Mr. Talbot connected to the company?"

"Well, I'm not sure exactly. I think he does some kind of work for Mainline, maybe sales... I dunno.

But he's at almost every race and he hangs around the company booths. I seen him talking to potential customers and stuff."

"And what did he say to you?" Rosa asked. "Important information about the races?"

"Nah. He thinks the sign should go a bit higher."

"Oh. So, you're saying you don't actually know what he does?"

Pete Johansson just shrugged narrow shoulders. "No, sorry, miss."

Rosa thanked the young man and turned away. At least she had gotten a name. She looked for the figure of Cy Talbot and saw him still standing by the coffee machine. He removed a set of keys from his pocket and walked briskly to the exit doors. Rosa hurried to catch up with him.

Once outside, Mr. Talbot walked purposefully toward the paved parking lot beside the hall, stopping when he got to a black Ford sedan. He inserted the key into the door.

"Mr. Talbot!" Rosa called. He stopped and regarded her curiously as she approached.

"Whew, you walk pretty fast," Rosa said waving her notepad.

"Do I know you, miss?"

Rosa reverted to her English accent. "No, I don't

suppose so. My name is Kate Thorpe, and I am a correspondent for a magazine called..." her mind worked quickly, "*Fast Tracks.*"

"Never heard of it."

"We are based in London. We normally feature stories on Formula One racing in Europe, but our chief editor thought it would be good to do a story on the phenomenon of stock car racing in America. I've been to several races already. Intriguing material, really."

"I'm not sure what that has to do with me." He glowered at her. "How do you know my name?"

"I'm a journalist, Mr. Talbot. It's my job to know these things."

He opened his car door. "I have nothing to say. I'm sorry."

"Just a comment please, Mr. Talbot." Rosa decided to go out on a limb. "Give me something juicy for our avid readers in London."

The man sighed. "Okay, I'll bite."

"Some people have accused companies like Mainline of taking part in race fixing. What do you make of that, and do you think that played any part in the race here?"

"You've got some nerve." His mouth formed a thin line.

"Have I? How's that?"

"What did you say your name was again?" He stepped closer. The menace in his eyes was unmistakable.

"Kate Thorpe."

"Let me give you some advice, Miss Thorpe. Do your story on stock car racing, but you should stop trying to dig up the desert dirt. I don't know what it's like in jolly old England, but here in California, if you turn over the wrong stone you might find a scorpion or two."

He slammed the door closed and pulled out of the stall. Rosa noticed that the metal licence plate holder had the words *Premier Auto Rental-Santa Bonita* engraved on it.

"We'll see about that," she said to herself as the black Ford roared off.

Back in the hall, Rosa picked up the payphone in the foyer and dialed the number of the Santa Bonita Police Department. There was no answer at Miguel's desk so she rang Sanchez's phone. His gravelly voice crackled over the line.

"Yeah, Miguel is not in right now, but lucky you. You got me instead. What can I do for my favourite Kiwi detective?"

"I think you might mean *Limey,* though it's not exactly polite."

"Okay, okay. I took a shot and missed." He chuckled again. "What's up?"

"I might have something interesting regarding the case, but perhaps you could help check something out for me?"

"No problemo."

Rosa could hear him rummaging through his desk drawer, probably looking for a pen and notepad. "Okay shoot."

19

The Santa Bonita Town Hall was one of the city's oldest buildings. The plaque hanging by the wooden front doors read, EST. 1836. It had almost been torn down in 1949, after a small fire in the hall's kitchen, but Aunt Louisa had led the charge to preserve it as a historic building.

Rosa couldn't help but find the concept of a 120-year-old building being considered ancient when the house she'd grown up in was more than twice that age. Some structures in Britain dated back to Roman times.

It wasn't the first time Rosa had been to a dance in this hall; she'd attended a few during her teen years while escaping the dangers of World War Two in England. Once again, Miguel was a major feature in her memories — another reason to leave for Galveston with Larry.

Dancing was a favorite pastime of her parents, and Rosa had grown up going to dances and balls. After the strenuous pursuit of clues to break the Downing case, Rosa was ready for an evening of fun.

When the band climbed onto the stage, Rosa's heart skipped a beat, thinking that the lead singer was Miguel, but thankfully, he was only similar in profile. One reason Rosa had agreed to accompany Larry to this dance was that Miguel's band, Mick and the Beat Boys, weren't scheduled to play.

The hall was soon filled with the vibration of loud rock and roll guitar riffs, the band proving to excel at all of the day's hits such as "Be-Bop-a-Lula" and "Why Do Fools Fall in Love."

As Larry drew her to the dance floor, his eyes twinkled as he said, "You look lovely tonight, Miss Reed."

Rosa had taken extra care with her choice of dress, a cherry-red chiffon with a full, netted petticoat, narrow waist, and slender shoulder straps. Gold sequins embellished the bodice, and Rosa had chosen gold teardrop earrings to go with the outfit.

"Thank you, Dr. Rayburn," she returned lightly. "You look dapper as well."

Rosa didn't recognize many dancers apart from Gloria, who'd come with her current squeeze, Ben Applebaum, a fellow not on Aunt Louisa's list of acceptable future sons-in-law. Clarence—with other young men dressed in white shirts with black ties, high-waisted gabardine slacks, and slicked-back hair —huddled by the bar, just out for a laugh and in search of a pretty girl to dance with.

The number slowed, and Larry pulled Rosa closer. "About Galveston, I've started packing."

"I see." Rosa stared up at Larry. "And when you see me there, where exactly am I living?"

Larry's lip tugged up crookedly. "Well, that would be up to you. My sister has a spare room, or I could find you a boarding house."

"A boarding house!" Rosa had never lived in anything that wasn't a family home, and they'd all been rather large ones at that. Not that she was opposed to smaller dwellings, but a boarding house seemed rather extreme.

"No, forget that. Not a boarding house. I don't know where that came from." Larry spun her around, then whispered in her ear.

"You could always stay with me."

Despite herself, Rosa's heart hammered in her chest, but not as one would expect—not with the thrill of new love, but rather in dismay that Larry would be so casual when he was asking such a big thing of her.

How ironic that the marriage proposal she desired from one man was nowhere to be found when another man, Winston, couldn't stop himself from proposing. *Oh, the poetic tragedy of life!*

Not trusting her emotions, Rosa turned back to safer ground. "Do you have news about Rufus Downing's postmortem?"

Larry pulled back with a sniff. "Uh, no. I'll have the report ready in the morning."

Her question had poured cold water on Larry's enthusiasm for dancing, and when the number ended, he led her back to their table.

"Can I get you another drink?" he asked.

"A rum and coke would be nice."

Rosa stared at the door, half expecting Miguel to walk through, and if she was honest with herself, hoping that he would.

How wretched was she! *Drat that man!*

Larry returned with their drinks, his smile tame, his eyes without their normal twinkle. "You keep looking at the door. Are you expecting someone?"

As if she'd been caught out, Rosa felt her cheeks

flush. "No. I'm only wondering why they don't prop it open. It's rather warm in here."

"The windows are open, and the fans are running."

"Yes, well, it must just be me."

Rosa sipped her drink, envying the carefree laughter coming from Gloria as she danced with Ben. What would Gloria do if Ben suddenly asked her to move away with him? Probably laugh in his face.

Were Aunt Louisa and Grandma Sally right? Was Larry Rayburn asking too much of her?

Then, worse than if Miguel had been singing with the band, he entered the hall with a gorgeous brunette on his arm. Rosa felt her breath escape her, and she quickly hid her distress by sipping on her drink. Miguel's dark-eyed gaze found hers, and he lifted a hand, acknowledging her and Larry. But instead of joining them, Miguel took the girl's hand and led her to the dance floor. Rosa's heart broke as he smiled at his dance partner, the dimples she loved so dearly on display for the benefit of someone else.

"That's Ruth Baker," Larry offered. "She's a nurse at the hospital."

"She seems lovely."

"She is."

Rosa's gaze snapped to Larry as he watched the eye-catching girl dance, and in that instant, knew that Miss Baker and Larry had dated in the past.

The question was, why hadn't it worked out? Why had Larry set his eyes on Rosa instead?

The band played too loudly for those questions, and Rosa didn't think she wanted to know the answers to them anyway. She grabbed Larry's hand. "Let's dance."

Larry's smile returned, and he drew her to the dance floor. Determined not to let her eyes seek Miguel and his new girl, she kept her gaze firmly on Larry.

Not only that, in that instant, Rosa decided. She would go to Galveston.

20

*I*n place of breakfast the next morning, Rosa popped a couple of aspirin.

"Are you feeling okay, Miss Rosa," Señora Gomez asked.

"I'm afraid I had one drink too many at the dance last night."

"Ah, dancing makes you thirsty, *si*? Makes you want to drink more."

"Yes, but water would be better than rum." Rosa chuckled then winced. The sound of her voice felt as if an ice pick pierced her brain. Although she hadn't drunk so much that she didn't remember. The image of Miguel and Ruth dancing together was etched deeply in her brain. No, she had not kept her inner vow not to stare at the smart-looking couple, but she did hope that Larry hadn't noticed.

Oh dear.

Rosa also remembered deciding to go to Galveston, but she was very glad that despite getting tipsy, she had made no declarations to Larry. She thought she'd still like to go, though. Santa Bonita was feeling too small. She was a big-city girl at heart, having mostly grown up in London. Getting lost in a city like Galveston where there were no overprotective and opinionated relatives, and especially no ghosts of past romances, seemed like just what the doctor ordered.

Larry had said he'd have a report on Rufus Downing's postmortem, so Rosa's first stop was the hospital morgue. She could only hope that Nurse Baker wasn't working.

When she saw Dr. Philpott at his desk, Rosa ducked in to say hello.

"No kitty cat today?" the chief medical examiner asked.

"He's taking a day off."

Dr. Philpott tapped a file on his desk. "If you're looking for the Downing report, I have it here."

"Yes, I'd love to see it, if you don't mind."

"Well, normally, I only report to the police, but

Detective Belmonte has given me carte-blanche permission to answer whatever questions you have."

"The police and I cooperate as much as we can," Rosa said. Her gaze moved to Larry's empty office and scoured the empty hall.

"Looking for Dr. Rayburn, are you?"

"Is he in?"

"Stepped out for a bit of personal business."

Rosa felt a twinge of disappointment. Now that she'd decided to go to Galveston, her original uncertainty was falling away and excitement about a new adventure brewed.

"He's leaving soon," Dr. Philpott continued. "We'll miss him." He winked, then added, "I'm sure we're not alone, but from what I understand, you may not be missing one another for long."

Rosa's mood soured. Why did Larry keep telling people she was moving to Galveston when she hadn't even confirmed it to him yet herself? Especially after he had apologized for it once already.

She shook her unease off with a slow inhale, motioned to the file on Dr. Philpott's desk, and asked, "What have you found?"

"Rufus Downing had no alcohol at all in his blood."

"Is that so?"

"It is, though his clothes, his body, they reeked of whiskey or some kind of alcohol."

"Someone poured that on him to make it look like he was drunk," Rosa said.

A third voice responded, "I came to the same conclusion."

Rosa spun at the sound of Miguel's voice. Her mind told her to be steady, but her heart, beating madly, betrayed her. "Hello, Miguel."

Miguel pinned her with his dark-eyed gaze. "Hiya, Rosa."

Against her will, Rosa found herself dry-swallowing. Could Miguel see how he affected her? Did he care...even a little?

Not if Rosa could go by Ruth Baker. She certainly wasn't going to ask him about her.

Forcing her voice back to neutral, she said to both men, "Did the killer think you wouldn't check for alcohol in the blood or even do an autopsy at all?"

"Maybe the culprit thought the actual cause of death would deter us," Dr. Philpott said. "The front hood of the car was pushed up through the windshield and into the front seat, nearly cutting his head clean off." He stopped for a moment. "Sorry, I don't mean to put you off your lunch."

"No problem," Rosa said, though the mental

image did make a shiver shoot through her. "I've seen my fair share of dead bodies. Anyway, I think I know how it all happened."

Miguel lifted his chin. "Oh? How so?"

"Yesterday, at the lookout, I stayed behind after everyone else had left."

Miguel's eyes narrowed with disapproval, but he remained silent.

Rosa continued, "Diego got away from me, and I had to chase him down the ravine where he then decided to climb a tree."

One of Miguel's gorgeous dimples made an appearance as he fought a smirk. "Don't tell me you climbed a tree?"

"Indeed. A pine."

The second dimple showed. "And the point of your story?"

"From my position in the tree, I could see the entire flattened view of the cliffside from top to bottom. The surface wasn't all bare rock, but, although it was sparse, there was a certain amount of grass and thistle growing between the cracks."

"And?"

Rosa couldn't help but feel a mite irritated by his interruption.

"And...at high speeds, which everyone is

assuming Rufus Downing was driving at, a car would launch into the air, especially off that point of the embankment, before hitting the ground and the subsequent trees that stopped it."

"Are you saying the car didn't gain air?" Miguel asked. "I know there weren't any skid marks, but that just means Rufus Downing didn't bother to hit the brakes. It's possible he decided to end his own life."

"From my perch in the tree, I could see two tracks from the four wheels as the car went over the edge. The grass was torn and flattened where the tires went down, leaving a faint but definite trail. Much of the tall thistle and weed tops were torn off between the two sets of tracks, no doubt from getting caught in the car's undercarriage. All this would be almost impossible to notice from the ground, unless you were specifically looking for it, because of the foliage's sparseness. But when I saw it from my vantage point in the tree, it was obvious. I then investigated more closely with my magnifying glass. The trail of broken weeds and compacted grass begins right at the very top." She paused for a moment as understanding came into Miguel's eyes

Rosa continued, "Rufus's car wasn't moving fast, but slowly, breaking foliage as it went. I believe someone knocked Rufus out and poured alcohol on him to make him appear as if he were driving drunk. At the most dangerous curve of the highway, the driver jumped out of the car as it rolled along at a low speed, letting it go over the edge. He probably sat Rufus right next to him in the middle of the seat."

"That would make it look like he was behind the wheel when the car went over," Dr. Philpott said.

"Now, that would have been a bit daring," Miguel said. "Jumping from a moving car, even at a slow speed, is dangerous. The driver could have been easily injured."

"And as far as knocking the victim out, the decedent had numerous contusions," Dr. Philpott said. "If a person didn't know better, it would be natural to assume they all came from a wreck like this one."

Miguel turned to Rosa. "You're certain about the tracks?"

"I am. I took photographs from the tree and also from up close."

Miguel grimaced. "I can't believe we missed that."

"I would've missed it too," Rosa offered, "if it wasn't for Diego."

"Deputy Diego strikes again," Miguel said with a chuckle.

Rosa thanked Dr. Philpott and turned to leave, surprised when Miguel walked out with her.

"What are you going to do now?" he asked.

She tilted her head and raised a brow.

"I mean, it appears that you are still working for your deceased client," Miguel continued. "We might as well help one another if we can."

Rosa agreed. She and Miguel might not be friends, but that would be no excuse for not being friendly.

"I thought I'd head to the convention. Perhaps, someone there might be able to shed more light on the puzzle."

"I had the same thought. I have to head back to the station first, but maybe I'll see you there."

By now, the convention was in full swing. The street was full of cars, forcing Rosa to park her Corvette several blocks away. This time, there was a line to get into the place, and it took ten minutes before she was finally inside.

The hall was crammed with people milling about, taking pictures, and talking to the display keepers. Carl Ryder, dressed in his white racing overalls, was at a kiosk signing autographs. Other men, dressed in racer's overalls, sat nearby and signed autographs, but Rosa didn't recognize them. Her gaze eventually landed on Miguel and Detective Sanchez, who stood beside the Hudson Hornet display car, eating hot dogs and admiring the engine compartment.

"Must be nice being a police detective," Rosa quipped. "You fellas work so hard. You must be exhausted. Maybe you should sit down for a bit. I can bring you some water."

"Ha ha," Miguel replied.

Detective Sanchez held up his hot dog and sang the well-known rhyming slogan, "You get the protein you require, from wieners made by Oscar Mayer."

Rosa's stomach rebelled at the offer, still uneasy from the dance, and she cringed. "Don't get any mustard or ketchup on your new shirt." Sanchez wore a neatly pressed short-sleeved shirt with a smart-looking blue tie. "Carlotta wouldn't be pleased."

Rosa noticed a sudden scowl on Miguel's face.

Ignoring his disapproval, Rosa kept her attention on Detective Sanchez. "Did she help you pick it out?"

"Uh-huh," he said with a full mouth. "The tie too."

"There's Chester Freemont." Miguel pointed over to where the NASCAR organizer was chatting with a group of racing fans beside one of the other display cars. "He was sure surprised when we cornered him on his Asheville roots."

"Not too happy," Sanchez mumbled, his mouth full of food. "Thanks for the tip on that, Rosa, by the way."

"Anyway," Miguel continued, "he was reluctant, but he eventually spilled those beans. It turns out his father was an infamous criminal in the thirties and even into the forties. He was a con artist who swindled money from many people through various get-rich-quick schemes that he instigated. The name Freemont, apparently, is a dirty word in a lot of places in North Carolina. Mr. Freemont senior died in a Raleigh prison ten years ago."

Sanchez flicked a few crumbs away from his thick stomach. "A guy has to wonder if a penchant for dirty dealings was passed from father to son."

"Did you ask him about race fixing?" Rosa asked.

Miguel nodded. "He denied it, of course."

"We'll check out his story about the walk on the beach yesterday morning," Sanchez offered. "If he's telling the truth, then someone must have seen him from above the beach or at one of the concessions

along the boardwalk." He pointed to the Mainline
Shocks and Struts kiosk. "Is that Cy Talbot? He
looks like a mean *hombre*."

Rosa nodded. "It is, but he's completely changed
his outfit." Mr. Talbot now wore a white T-shirt with
the Mainline Shocks and Struts logo emblazoned on
the front, along with grey slacks and brown leather
shoes. He was hatless, revealing thinning gray hair.
Because of the new outfit, it was easy to see that the
man was in top shape with muscular arms and shoulders. He held what looked to Rosa like a black,
painted shock absorber of some kind. With a surly
expression, his eyes slowly scanned the room.

"It almost looks like he wants to hit someone
with that thing," Sanchez remarked.

"I don't think I'd have much confidence in his
salesmanship skills with a mean look like that,"
Miguel said. "I'm guessing his role in the sales
department is a front."

Sanchez shifted his weight and crossed his arms.
"Yeah, I checked him out with the Los Angeles
precinct. He's been on their radar for a while. Loan
sharking and money laundering. They suspect him
of being involved in race bribing for Mainline Shocks
and Struts. The police suspect the company has ties
to the West Coast Mafia."

"The plot thickens," Rosa said.

Sanchez grinned. "I like to say the tortilla soup thickens. But here's the thing: it doesn't look like he was in town for the race."

"We checked with the car rental company," Miguel added. "He didn't pick up the car until yesterday. Premier Auto Rentals always request that information from out-of-town customers if they plan to use the car in town here, so we called the hotel and they confirmed that he only arrived yesterday mid-afternoon."

Rosa braced her hands on her hips. "Well, then what on earth did I hear them talking about?"

"My guess," Sanchez said, "is they were talking about the last big NASCAR race in Gardena. The detective in Los Angeles, who is a racing fan, told me that NASCAR has strict policies against race fixing, but just like any other sport, it's hard to prove when it happens. A few weeks ago there was a race in Gardena, one of the few races that the Downings were *not* a part of, and the guy who was favored to win..." He turned and pointed to the "Rapid Reggie" sign. "... didn't win. Apparently, he dominated the race until the last few laps and then slid back into second place."

The trio turned and regarded the sandy-haired

man who stood beside the big sign featuring his like-
ness. He was signing autographs and giving away
baseball caps that had his name embroidered on the
brim. The driver glanced across the room at Cy
Talbot and nodded his head. They obviously knew
each other.

Rosa frowned. "I guess you could be right about
that conversation. It could have been about race
fixing, but not necessarily the race we had here."
Flicking her wrist, she stared at her watch. "The next
race starts in a few hours."

"Ladies and gentlemen, can I have your attention, please?" The voice of Chester Freemont came
over the speaker system. All eyes turned to the
NASCAR official who was wearing blue-denim
trousers and a white, collared short-sleeve shirt with
the NASCAR insignia emblazoned on one of the
front pockets. Standing behind a small podium and
with a big smile on his face, he removed a piece of
paper from his breast pocket and unfolded it. He
cleared his throat and leaned forward into the small
microphone.

"Howdy, everyone. My name is Chester
Freemont, and I am the NASCAR representative for
today's event. Now, I am not accustomed to
speeches. I prefer spending my time at the racetrack,

but we'll be heading there soon, so don't worry." There were murmurs of excitement from the crowd.

"I would like to thank all the people who have helped out with this event." He mentioned a long list of people that Rosa did not recognize. "The first thing I want to do today is to pay tribute to these two drivers you see pictured here." He gestured to the portraits of the Downing brothers, one on either side of him.

"It is just inconceivable that these two young men, so full of promise, could have been taken from us in the same week, and both in this lovely city. The police have ruled the deaths as homicide, and we all pray for the speedy resolution to this terrible injustice." He shuffled his papers and cleared his throat again. "Of course, the Downing name is not unknown to any of us who follow or are involved in the wonderful sport of stock car racing..."

As Chester Freemont continued with his speech, Rosa scanned the room for the sign of the Stetson hat worn by T-Bone Rafferty. Given their history, she wondered what his reaction would be to this tribute to the Downing brothers.

She wandered through the crowd to the back of the room just in time to see the retreating form of T-Bone Rafferty moving through the glass exit doors,

likely leaving for the track. She followed him to the
doors and watched as he walked down the sidewalk.

Rosa noticed something odd. T-Bone Rafferty
had a heavy limp, favoring his left leg. She was sure
she would have noticed that had it been there before.

*An injury from diving out of a moving car,
perhaps?*

BEFORE ROSA REALIZED what she was doing, she
was outside following T-Bone Rafferty. Unfortunately, his car was parked closer to the venue than
hers, and when she got to her Corvette, her opportunity to follow the curious man was lost.

Would he go directly to the track? It was a little
early for that, and Rosa reasoned that he might head
to Ricky's Garage first, which was only a few blocks
away. By the time Chuck Berry's hit song, "May-
belline," had played on the radio—one of many car-
themed songs played in light of the coming race—
Rosa had pulled up close to the garage. All the bay
doors were closed, and the lights were off.

Rosa sighed and put the car into gear to drive on,
but as she looked over her right shoulder, she noticed
that both the gym that the garage owner had previ-
ously pointed out to her, and the Waffle House next

to it were open for business. She stared at the two businesses with her motor running for a moment before finally turning off her car and climbing out.

She crossed the street and approached the gym. There weren't many in Santa Bonita. The only other one she knew of was called Jimmy Gym's Fitness Club. She had been there once a few months ago to question a murder suspect—her first murder case upon returning to Santa Bonita from England. The sign on the door of this club read Sam's Gym. She entered a reception area that had a counter facing the entry door and several cloth chairs. There was no one at the counter, but there was a small bell. A moment after ringing it, a well-built young man in his thirties stepped around the corner.

"Yes, can I help you?"

Rosa introduced herself and showed her card. "I am investigating a matter, and I wonder if I could trouble you with a few questions."

The man looked surprised. "Of course. How can I help?"

"I understand you have a regular client that comes in. He's tall, middle-aged, and has a scar on his left cheek."

"That would be Mr. Rafferty. He's involved with racing."

"Yes, that's right. So, he's been coming in here every morning?"

"You bet. Stays for about an hour. He's one of our older clients, but in pretty good shape, I'd say."

"Do you remember if he was here yesterday morning? Probably, first thing in the morning?"

"I wasn't in that day. Sometimes there's no one here operating the front desk first thing in the morning, but there's a sign-in list. I'll check." He reached under the counter, brought out a large clipboard, and ran his finger down the list after turning a page. "Here he is. Yeah, he signed in at eight thirty like usual."

"And when did he leave?"

"I couldn't tell you. But you can check next door, though. He always goes for breakfast at the Waffle House right after he leaves here."

Rosa thanked the man and went into the restaurant. It was much larger than it looked from the outside and was almost full. The wood-paneled walls and maple-wood floors offered a warm atmosphere. The smell of coffee and waffles with syrup was pervasive, and Rosa's stomach suddenly came alive

"Welcome!" A friendly young lady with a large glass coffee pot approached. "Just pick an empty seat anywhere."

"I only have a quick question. Well, two."

The waitress smoothed out her white apron with her free hand. "Go on."

"Were you working here yesterday morning?"

"Uh-huh. Why?"

"My name's Rosa Reed, and I'm a private investigator. I'm looking for a Mr. Rafferty. He's tall, middle-aged, usually wears a Stetson. He has a faded scar on his left cheek."

"I know him." Her brow crumpled. "Is he in trouble?"

Rosa wasn't sure if he was *in* trouble or if he *was* trouble. She smiled without answering.

"Was he here yesterday morning?"

"He was, but he didn't stay for his usual waffle and eggs special. Normally, he stays awhile afterward, sipping coffee and reading his newspapers."

"You mean he came in but didn't eat anything?"

"Uh-huh." She pointed to a payphone on the wall immediately to the left of the entrance. "He only used that phone."

A cork bulletin board attached to the wall beside the telephone was covered in handwritten announcements and business cards.

"Then he just walked through the restaurant and went out the rear door," the waitress continued. "Now that I think about it, it was kind of strange."

"Mr. Rafferty had never done that before?"

"Gosh no, never. The funny thing is, he came in again through the rear entrance a couple of hours later, strolled right on through and left through the front door." She glanced at her wristwatch. "Did you have another question?"

"Oh, yes," Rosa said with a smile. "I'd like to order a plate of pancakes." She pointed to a free table by the window. "I'll sit there."

"Blueberry, buttermilk, or regular?"

"Buttermilk."

As Rosa waited, she took a seat and, deep in thought, stared out the window. The work bays of Ricky's Garage would be visible from this vantage point. Whoever was working in the garage had a clear view of both the gym and the restaurant's entrances.

Had he chosen these businesses because of that?

Somewhat perplexed, Rosa glanced at the telephone, trying to mentally retrace Mr. Rafferty's steps. She meandered over, her eyes focused on the bulletin board.

Most notes were handwritten advertisements for everything from instrument lessons to garage sales, and business cards offering various services. There wasn't enough room on the board for them all, and some were tacked on over each other. Out of curiosity, she scanned the board. Near the bottom, tacked on top of a small stack of cards, was a plain-white handwritten card that read "Randy's Reptiles".

Rosa unpinned the card and stuck the pin back onto those underneath. The card looked new and uncreased. Rosa guessed that whoever Randy was, he'd been in the Waffle House recently as his card had been pinned to the top of a stack, perhaps to replace one picked up by a killer sometime before the race. That it was handwritten suggested that the business was not one widely advertised in all the usual places like a phone book or the classified ads.

Rosa picked up the receiver and dialed the number.

The phone rang five times. Rosa was about to hang up when she heard a man's voice. "Hello?"

"Oh, hello. Is that Randy's Reptiles?" Rosa affected her best Queen's English. She wanted her accent to sound as British as possible and to, hopefully, sound older than she was.

"Who's asking?"

"My name is Mrs. Thornby. My husband and I have recently retired and have moved here from

London. Both of us have a great interest in reptiles, well *snakes* to be precise, Mr....uh Randy. The long and short of it is that we want to build a menagerie, so to speak, on our newly acquired ranch. We moved to California specifically for that purpose."

"From England, huh?"

"Yes, we are just now at a lovely waffle house, and I noticed your card on the wall. I haven't shown it to my husband, William, yet. He's sitting over there enjoying his waffles. Anyway, unlike England, there are a lot of interesting snakes in America. We would be very interested to know what kind of snakes you have for sale. Particularly those of the venomous kind."

"It's illegal to sell venomous snakes," the man said gruffly.

"*What*? Oh no! We didn't realize that. How awful. We shall have to rethink our strategy, perhaps. Oh my, William will be upset. We had planned to buy at least six or seven snakes of the more, shall we say, *villainous* variety. We thought it very 'Wild West,' you see. Of course, we would keep them penned up and far from any public."

"Six or seven, you say?"

"Yes, and we have a large budget set aside. Oh, what a disappointment."

There was a moment of silence on the phone before the man responded. "Tell you what. I may be of some help to you. I have a few snakes that you may find interesting, maybe even a few uh...'villainous' ones. I keep a few out back just for my own amusement, you understand. We might be able to strike a deal."

"Oh, that would be marvelous. We aren't looking for large snakes. Nothing like a king cobra or anything like that. And they don't necessarily have to be local. We hope to fill our collection with snakes from various parts of this grand country."

"I have a few you might like, Mrs. Thornby. Including one of the smaller poisonous snakes in America."

"Would that be the *Sistrurus Miliarius?* The infamous pygmy rattler?"

"Seems to be a popular snake. Well, let's just say, I think I can help you."

"Jolly good!"

The man gave an address about ten miles southeast of town. "Bring your husband and come on out and see me. You have to understand, though, if someone ever asks where you got them—"

"Of course. Mum's the word."

"The laws against selling poisonous snakes are

on the books but rarely enforced. Neither are the laws against owning them. You still have to be a bit careful," he cautioned.

"Discretion is paramount. I understand completely, sir. Our collection will never be for public viewing."

Rosa hung up the phone and considered her next move. She still didn't know who Mr. Rafferty had called yesterday morning and could only guess he'd contacted Randy's Reptiles. Rosa glanced at her wristwatch. The exhibition race started in an hour. If she didn't hurry, she would miss it. Thankfully, her stack of pancakes had just arrived.

21

*H*oping to find Miguel at the race, Rosa paid her entrance fee and joined the throng. The drivers stood on a podium, and Rosa—having squeezed through to a place along the fence—made a show of waving. Seeing her, the men waved back, and though she wasn't any different from the other excited spectators who waved and hooted, she did catch T-Bone Rafferty's eye.

"Mr. Rafferty," she yelled. "I know about Randy's Reptiles."

T-Bone frowned.

Just to ensure that he'd heard her, she yelled it again. "Randy's Reptiles."

If she was right, and Mr. Rafferty had made a

call to Randy in the near past, then he should look good and nervous right about now. She wanted to see his reaction.

"What's all the shouting about?"

Rosa turned to the voice she knew so well and offered a half-smile to Miguel. "I think Mr. Rafferty might be our man."

"How so?"

Rosa described her findings at the gym and Waffle House and her phone call to Randy's Reptiles. "On further investigation, I think you'll find that's where our murder weapon came from."

"Sounds suspicious, all right," Miguel said. "But who did he phone that morning?"

"Good question," Rosa answered. "But we now know that he had time on Wednesday to murder Rufus Downing. He likely went into the restaurant just to give himself an alibi. The men in the garage wouldn't have known the difference from his routine. They would've seen him go in there at the same time as usual and come out the same time too. All he had to do was park his car at the back of the restaurant."

Mr. Stober's voice came over the loudspeaker, directing the drivers to go to their cars. T-Bone Rafferty's eyes darted in Rosa's direction, and his frown deepened as he registered Miguel beside her.

"I'm going to call dispatch," Miguel said as he stepped away. "We may need backup when the race is over."

The now-familiar sound of roaring engines and a cheering crowd grew, and as Rosa looked over to the track, she could make out the form of Rick Stober standing in the start marshal's tower.

The backup cruisers arrived as the racers made their third trip around the track with T-Bone Rafferty, driving a brightly painted red Ford with the number fourteen on the door, in the lead.

Miguel appeared once again at Rosa's side. "What did I miss?"

"Nothing out of the ordinary," Rosa said, a moment too soon. To the crowd's amazement, instead of making the next bend, Mr. Rafferty crashed through the wooden barricade that served as an entry point for racing cars and service vehicles, shredded plywood flying in pieces.

T-Bone Rafferty, wearing a helmet, yelled at the top of his lungs. "Yeehaw!"

"*Por todos los Santos!*" Miguel spat.

As he pushed through the crowds to where his cruiser was parked, Rosa followed in his wake.

Since Detective Sanchez was caught in the

crowd and not at Miguel's side, Rosa jumped into the front seat.

Miguel's eyes were fierce as he grabbed the magnetic strobe light from under the dashboard and threw it on top of the car. "Hang on!" he shouted as he backed out the vehicle, threw it into forward gear, and stomped on the accelerator. Rocks and gravel went flying as the car fishtailed and then straightened out. Rosa hung on to the door's handgrip for dear life as Miguel picked up the radio unit's microphone.

"Attention all units, attention all units. This is Detective Belmonte in car number one in pursuit of a...a... racing car!" He shot a wild look at Rosa then keyed the microphone. "It's a red-and-white Ford with the number fourteen on the door, and it's moving fast!"

Rosa gulped as she felt the color drain from her face. This was the second time in a month she had been involved in a high-speed chase. The last one ended with her almost rolling her car and crashing into the back of a farm vehicle. She was not eager to get into another one.

"I wonder what tipped him off," Miguel said, his knuckles turning white against the black steering wheel.

Rosa glared back. "I wanted him to know that I knew or to think that I knew, and that there *was* something to know, which clearly there was."

Miguel shot her a wild, confused look.

"Well, I didn't think he would..." She threw up her hands. "You know, make a *run* for it."

"I think the backup cruisers, driving up as the race started, just sealed the deal," Miguel said.

Suddenly, the stock car left the right lane and veered directly into the path of an oncoming police car. Avoiding a deadly collision, the police cruiser swerved to its left and dove into a small irrigation ditch filled with muddy water where it stalled, bogged down in heavy mud.

Meanwhile, T-Bone Rafferty turned left onto the Coast Highway with tires squealing. Blue-colored smoke filled the air as he sped south toward the town of Kerrisville. Rosa looked behind and saw that the three cruisers which had been parked at the race-track were in pursuit far in the distance. The smell of burned rubber assailed her nostrils.

Miguel turned onto the highway with the siren sounding and the light flashing and gunned the car again as the engine roared. Rosa knew this stretch of highway—it was winding and hilly as it snaked through the foothills south of Santa Bonita, never straying too far from the Pacific Ocean below. It was a road where it behooved one to pay attention to the posted speed limits. At high speeds, it could be downright treacherous.

Rosa glanced at the speedometer to see the needle approaching eighty miles an hour.

"Seat belt!" Miguel shouted as he pointed to the seatbelt beside her. He kept his eyes on the road.

Rosa was glad to see a small, chromed hook mechanism that must have been a special option installed on the "police package" cars. She reached to her right and found the metal buckle and snapped herself in.

With one hand on the wheel, Miguel found the buckle to his left and wrapped the belt across himself. Rosa reached over and snapped him in just as he pressed the brake pedal to enter a curve with tires squealing. As they came out of the curve, Rosa could see the stock car, in the distance, coming upon a much slower vehicle. It weaved back and forth behind the slower car impatiently.

"We got him!" Miguel shouted, even though they were still a long way off. However, there was a steady flow of oncoming traffic and a blind corner coming up, trapping the stock car between the police car and the car in front. On the right was a narrow, dirt shoulder with a metal guardrail. Down below, the ocean crashed into a rugged, rocky shoreline.

Unexpectedly, the stock car accelerated right and drove onto the dirt shoulder, even though it didn't look to Rosa that there was enough room to allow a car to pass. But impossibly, the red Ford thundered by the car in front of it with sparks flying off its right side from the guardrail. The sound of screeching metal could be heard above the roaring of the car's engine. The slower car swerved, the driver apparently realizing a madman was trying to pass on the wrong side.

"Unbelievable," Miguel muttered, his mouth hanging open.

The car up ahead must have finally noticed the flashing lights in the rearview mirror because it pulled over onto the shoulder. Miguel once again gunned the engine and tore past it.

The stock car was out of sight, and Miguel negotiated several connected curves through a densely forested area on both sides as the road continued at an incline. At each turn, the tires squealed. Miguel fought to find the right rhythm between braking, accelerating, and using momentum to come out of a curve at speed.

They finally came to a straight downhill stretch

and saw the red stock car far in front. To Rosa's dismay, it had gained considerable distance through the curves.

"How...?" Miguel seemed momentarily speechless as he shot a glance at Rosa.

Unable to imagine how anyone could negotiate those curves at greater speeds than Miguel was doing, she shrugged. It seemed impossible.

Miguel coaxed the car even faster until the speedometer read over ninety. The Kerrisville city limits sign came into view, and cars, seeing the flashing light, pulled over in droves as Miguel and Rosa sped toward the sleepy little town.

Miguel keyed the radio. "Attention dispatch. Be advised we are heading into Kerrisville in a high-speed pursuit. Please alert local units. Tell them to use extreme caution. This guy is dangerous."

After a moment, the radio crackled back to life. "Be advised all units. Please turn to channel number three to join Kerrisville police radio band."

Rosa reached down to turn the dial to the appropriate frequency.

"Thanks," Miguel said. "We're gonna get this guy."

"Attention all units, this is Detective Belmonte in

car number one," Miguel said into the microphone. "The suspect will probably follow along the most direct route through town to search for a secondary road leading into the mountains."

"Roger that," a voice returned. "This is Kerrisville Police dispatch. We will set up barricades."

The stock car had slowed but was still quite a way ahead of them. Thankfully, Kerrisville's main street was a long, straight stretch with only a couple of traffic lights. However, the dangerous nature of any high-speed chase through town was made clear when the stock car jumped onto a sidewalk to avoid hitting a large delivery truck. The race car tore through a fresh produce stand with carrots, mangoes, and cauliflowers exploding into the air like a bomb had gone off, with the vendor desperately diving sideways.

Rosa glanced at Miguel. His normally olive-colored face had paled at the sight of T-Bone Rafferty's car careening down the sidewalk, narrowly missing a few pedestrians before swerving back onto the street.

Dark eyes wide with near panic, Miguel shot a glance back at Rosa. "He's crazy!"

Ahead, they saw more dark smoke as the stock car slid sideways with all four tires chirping on the pavement. It swerved into a left turn just past an overhead sign that read San Marcos Pass.

"That's it. I hope they have some cars in place to block him," Miguel exclaimed. "If he gets into those mountains..."

The traffic thinned more as they blasted down the gently curved street through a business district that gave way to a more industrialized area with small factories and warehouses. Miguel tried to keep within sight of the stock car, but it required driving at an impossibly reckless speed, and after about thirty more seconds, they were losing sight of it.

Suddenly, a police barricade came into view far ahead. They had set up three police cars with lights flashing between two large brick buildings. Several officers stood at the rear of the cars with guns drawn, ready to leap out of the way if the madman in the stock car crashed into the barricade. There was no way to get past it.

Miguel slammed his hands on the wheel as he slowed. "Got him!"

Unfortunately, the ride was not over. In a move that stunned Rosa and would likely be discussed at the police office for months, the red Ford spun 180 degrees with the tires smoking and squealing in loud protest. Even as the vehicle's rear swung completely around, the car's momentum was still moving toward the police barricade with the rear wheels already spinning in the opposite direction. As the tires finally gained purchase, the rear bumper gently touched one of the police cruisers' side doors before the vehicle accelerated again and rocketed past Miguel and Rosa going in the opposite direction.

T-Bone Rafferty shouted through his open window, his eyes ferocious and locked on Miguel as he shot past. "*Haaawww!*"

Miguel hit his brakes and brought the cruiser to a stop. The officers appeared astonished at what they had just witnessed, all speechless.

Miguel blew out one long, shaky breath and then slammed into reverse. He got the car turned quickly and then gunned toward town. Rosa wondered when this day would end. Her stomach felt queasy, and she was more than a little light-headed. She had been in a few police chases in the past, but this one surpassed them all by far. The stories she had recently heard about the bootleg drivers of the Appalachians were not exaggerated.

They turned a corner just in time to see the stock car make yet another dramatic turn to the right as two patrol cars from Santa Bonita, followed by a police car from Kerrisville, sped after it. Miguel trailed them down a narrow back alley that looped around a large redbrick warehouse. Far ahead, Rosa saw the stock car cross an empty lot, crash through a wire fence and continue across a grass field, narrowly missing a drove of cows who clumsily moved out of the way as he sped past, the convoy of police cars in pursuit.

The stock car then climbed a small incline, crashed through a barbed-wire fence, and skidded onto a paved highway that headed up to the Santa Ynez Mountains' foothills. Unbelievably, T-Bone Rafferty had just successfully bypassed the police barricade.

With four cars now in immediate pursuit, including Miguel and Rosa's, the stock car disappeared around a bend. The harrowing chase continued for another five minutes, with the red Ford gaining more lead as the road continued to get steeper and more winding.

"This is hopeless," Miguel said as he entered another turn. "We can't keep this up; someone's going to get killed. We'll have to radio ahead to the next town. It will turn into a manhunt then."

Rosa was about to agree when, up ahead, a strange sight greeted them. T-Bone Rafferty leaned casually on the fender of the stock car where it was parked on the side of the road. He stood with his arms crossed, lazily smoking a cigarette. The hood of the Ford was crumpled open, and steam rose out of the engine compartment.

The pursuing police cars screeched to a stop, surrounding him. Officers jumped out with guns drawn, shouting for him to turn around and put his hands up. However, he calmly refused to move. As Rosa and Miguel climbed out of their car, Miguel motioned for the police to lower their weapons.

"He's not going anywhere," he shouted.

Rosa guessed that he would have done it already if he were the type to run into the woods. He wouldn't have gotten far even if he'd tried though, especially with an injured leg.

"Are you the pit crew?" T-Bone Rafferty chuckled dryly as Rosa and Miguel approached.

Rosa could hear a hissing and gurgling sound coming from the engine of the stock car.

"Looks like that last fence was one too many," Mr. Rafferty explained. "A piece of one of the wooden poles tore clear through the radiator." He looked at the engine and then shook his head as he dropped his cigarette and ground it out with his boot.

With narrowed eyes, he glared at them, his gravelly voice turning to a low growl. "Otherwise, there's no way in Hades you'da catch'ed me."

osa sat in the front passenger seat with Miguel as the police cruiser drove back to Santa Bonita. In the backseat sat T-Bone Rafferty. Miguel drove below the speed limit, which was just fine with Rosa, but it seemed to agitate their surly prisoner. They were followed by the police cars from Santa Bonita while the cruisers from Kerrisville stayed behind. Rosa was sure the officers would be talking about this day for a long time. Even instructional classes might be crafted and taught on the subject of high-speed dos and don'ts for the Kerrisville police force. The name of T-Bone Rafferty would be infamous.

"What's the matter, son? Are you still feelin' that

ol' adrenaline in your system?" came the scornful voice from the backseat. "Hard to calm down afterward, ain't it?"

Miguel's hands trembled on the wheel. He glared in the rearview mirror at the handcuffed man sitting behind the protective grille. "You could have killed innocent bystanders," he said.

Rosa could see him struggling to keep his voice even as he wrestled with emotions.

"Aw heck, Detective. I had it right in hand. It's all o' you amateurs that woulda done any killin' on the road. You shoulda just let it be. Old T-Bone woulda been someone else's problem by now, not yers. 'Sides, if you hadn't o' sent all those officers to the track, I wouldna gotten so nervous. On the other hand, it was fun to do one last run with the local law on my tail; it made me feel alive again, I gotta say."

Rosa could almost feel the heat of Miguel's anger rising in the front seat. The man had committed two murders in *his* town!

"How's your leg?" She decided it might be a good time to break into the conversation.

"What's that?"

"Your leg. You injured it while jumping out of Rufus Downing's rental car." She turned around to look at him.

"Ha. You're pretty perceptive, ain't you?" He narrowed his eyes as he regarded her. "Yeah, I twisted it a bit. Scraped my elbow too. Hurt like hell at the time. Didn't affect my driving none though, did it?" He chuckled. "Had you all chasin' around like rats in a maze."

"Your driving skills are impressive, all right," Rosa said, turning back to look at the road in front of them. "As I am sure your mechanical skills are as well. It's when it comes to hiding your own tracks, you fall woefully short, I'm afraid."

"What d'ya mean? I had you all running in circles!"

T-Bone Rafferty was the type of man that didn't like to be questioned, especially about what he thought he was good at. Men like him usually had loose tongues when their ego was challenged. She discreetly took her new Midgetape 44 recorder from her purse, turned the tiny microphone on, and put it on the seat beside her. Miguel shot her a surprised look.

"I disagree," Rosa said. "I think I had you figured out early on." *That's stretching the truth, but it might be a useful tactic.*

"You did not!"

"Well, I admit you had me guessing at first. But

when you tried to fake your alibi by walking through that restaurant instead of having breakfast, you blew it. You chose that place well beforehand, didn't you? You probably went there every morning just to establish it as a normal daily routine. It wasn't just their waffles that you liked, though; you liked their address, namely, right across the street from Ricky's Garage." She twisted to face toward their detainee. "Isn't that right?"

"Guilty as charged." He grinned.

She turned back to face the front. "That wasn't so clever, Mr. Rafferty. All I had to do was question the waitress. You were betting I wouldn't question your alibi by going in there. I am also guessing that's where you happened to see the business card; you know, the one for Randy's Reptiles? You took that card off the bulletin board, but you didn't think that Randy would replace that card once he saw it missing." She paused for effect. "Should I go on?"

"Impressive, Miss Reed. Yeah, go ahead. You're on a roll now."

"I am guessing that the person the waitress saw you on the phone with on Wednesday morning was Rufus Downing."

"You got it, smart lady." He nodded his head. "Keep going; this is very entertainin'."

"Well, I don't know for sure what you said to him. Maybe you called him to tell him you wanted to make amends. I mean, why else would he ever want to meet with you?"

"You guessed it right. Again!" He tapped on the metal grille and laughed. "Only I didn't want to make amends, did I? As if! I told him to meet me at my brother's ranch. I knew Philip would be gone for the day. It was easy to surprise Rufus from behind when he came into the house. I knocked him over the head with a shovel, dragged him into his car, poured whiskey on 'im. You gotta admit, that part was pretty clever."

Rosa made a mental note to get the police to search for that shovel. "It didn't fool anyone for long."

That seemed to perplex him for a moment. "Oh well, you gotta admit, it carries some irony, don't it? I didn't have any proper moonshine with me o' course, so I just used some of Philip's crap whiskey."

"It must have been hard to walk down that trail with an injured foot."

"Wasn't so bad. I only had to walk to the garage. As you know, it's on the outskirts of town. Later, I just took a cab back to the ranch."

"How did you know about the snakes? How did

you know Tucker Downing would have an allergic reaction?"

"Oh, you know about that too, huh? Yeah, that was a bit of a gamble in more ways than one. Especially after havin' paid a hundred bucks for that thing! I didn't know for sure *if* it would work and *when* that thing would bite 'im. It turned out just perfect, though, when the thing bit 'em right at the end there. Ha!"

Rosa and Miguel shared a look.

This man is cold-blooded.

"It was easy to sneak the snake into the backseat, though. I just released it from the thick cloth bag I had under my jacket. Those things sleep when you cover 'em up, ya know. I let it loose under the passenger seat in the back when the car was waitin' to be unloaded from the transport truck before the race."

T-Bone Rafferty seemed to get more talkative as he went, apparently relishing the opportunity to reveal his cleverness. "As for the allergy, now *that* part was truly fortuitous! I just happened to be in the *same* hospital on the *same* day with a bad appendix when he came in all puffed up an' purple tryin' to catch his breath. He just 'bout didn't make it. But when he did, I hatched my grand plan after hearing the doctor talkin' to the nurses out in the hallway. Turns out he and the *mini rattler* had struck up a lifelong 'agree to disagree' kind of arrangement." He chuckled again at his wit.

"I waited until this race in Santa Bonita because it carried a certain poetic justice. I am nothin' if not sentimental."

Miguel blew a long breath out of his cheeks and shook his head.

"S'matter, son? You don't think an ol' boy like me can have a highly developed sense of the poetic ironies in life?"

Miguel glared into the rearview mirror. "You'll have a good chance to write poetry where you're going."

"Maybe. On the other hand, maybe I got some lawyers that are smarter than you two put together. You'll be surprised at my capacity for denyin' everything I am telling you. Your little detective stories might be hard to prove outside o' this here car."

Rosa glanced down at her Midgetape 44. The *record* light, still red, indicated it was rolling. Miguel wisely kept his eyes straight ahead.

"Why did you do it?" Rosa asked. "I mean, your

brother, the *father* of the two young men killed on that stretch of highway, found it in his heart to realize it could have been an accident. Why couldn't you do the same? Why did you take on his offense?"

T-Bone Rafferty was uncharacteristically silent for a moment as he stared out the window at the Pacific Ocean. "Because someone had to. Philip's a good man, but he don't know the Downings like I do."

Turning, Rosa asked, "And how do you know them?"

He lifted a chin. "I believe I've already told you about my scar?"

Rosa nodded.

"Compliments of their ol' man. I've seen every one of the Downings cheat, steal, lie, and then finally kill those two boys!"

"Your brother told me that the police called it an accident," Rosa said.

"Yeah, well, *I* didn't. Sure, they might not have meant to kill them, but they meant to scare 'em somehow. The Downing brothers should have been put in jail for manslaughter at the very least. Instead, they got off scot-free." After a moment, he raised his voice to make a final point. "It's one thing to give the local authorities a story to cover your tracks, that's normal in the moonshine business, but it's quite another to cheat your own kind and to kill two innocent, fine young men."

23

*T*wo weeks after T-Bone Rafferty's arrest, Gloria was still crowing in the glory of having snatched the byline from Jake Wilson. Though it was too cool for swimming, the sunny fall day was perfect for sitting poolside, and Rosa relaxed in one of the lounge chairs as she listened to her cousin prattle on.

"Jake, uh, Mr. Wilson, hasn't forgiven me yet, and I hope he never does," Gloria said. Wearing a casual cotton day dress, she sipped from a cool piña colada. "That'll teach him for underestimating us females." She reached over to pat Rosa's arm and said for the hundredth time, "Thank you again for telling me T-Bone Rafferty had confessed. Mr.

Wilson's face when Mr. Mossman published my byline...I'll live on that high for weeks."

"You seem inordinately concerned by what Mr. Wilson thinks," Rosa said.

"I don't," Gloria protested. "It's just that he's such an arrogant cad."

"A handsome and charming arrogant cad," Rosa amended with a smile. She wasn't the only one in the house to notice that Ben Applebaum hadn't been mentioned in a good long while, much to Aunt Louisa's pleasure.

The sound of tennis balls bouncing in the distance caught Rosa's attention, and she smiled at the sight of Clarence teaching little Julie the elements of tennis. He'd had a small racket made and loosened the net in the middle of the court, causing it to sag. Julie's laughter carried in the wind, and it did Rosa's heart good to see the smile it brought to Clarence. Her cousin didn't have a lot that brought him joy in life. Young Julie was a gift to him—to them all—in that regard.

Aunt Louisa and Grandma Sally joined Rosa and Gloria on the terrace. Señora Gomez followed, a coffee tray in her hands.

In a large-brimmed hat generously decorated

with silk flowers, Grandma Sally said, "Sunday afternoons are my favorite time, having the family together like this."

"Not much more to do when all the stores are closed," Gloria said glibly.

"The people at the stores need a day off sometimes," Rosa offered.

"What? I don't go shopping *every day*!" Gloria waved her hand in the air dismissively.

At that, four women broke out in laughter.

Rosa's heart was warm with affection for her family. Was she *really* ready to leave them behind for Larry?

Larry! Rosa glanced at her watch. "Oh, I almost forgot. Larry's coming soon."

"What for?" Aunt Louisa said coolly. "To say goodbye?"

"Yes."

Rosa had agreed to meet Larry in Galveston after Christmas and he had offered his sister's room to her. He was driving out first thing the next morning.

Suddenly everyone remembered something... they had errands to run or were otherwise indisposed. Their reluctance to speak to Larry was a clear signal they didn't approve of him, as Grandma Sally had said, "sweeping their Rosa away."

Rosa made it to the front door just as Larry pulled in front. If nothing else, Larry was punctual. Rosa stepped outside to greet him. "Hello, Larry."

"Darlin'"

Larry kissed her deeply, his arms wrapping her tightly, and in that single moment she realized, finally, that she didn't feel *it*. She didn't love Larry, and if one left one's beloved family to move across the country with someone—someone who hadn't offered a proposal of marriage and the assumed commitment that comes with that—one should certainly feel *it*.

And if she didn't feel it now, it was unlikely she'd feel it after Christmas, when she and Larry would've been apart for several weeks.

"Darlin'? Is everything okay? You seem a little down."

Rosa placed her palms on Larry's chest. "Larry, I can't do it."

He stiffened. "Can't do what?"

"I can't move to Galveston. I'm not ready to leave my family, and I, well, I'm not in love with you. I thought, over time, if I came with you, my feelings would grow, and maybe they would, but..."

"I know, darlin'." He sighed, his chin dropping to his chest. "I saw it comin'. Have to be blind not to."

"I do wish you the best in Galveston," Rosa said. Despite knowing with a certainty she was doing the right thing, she choked up. "I hope we can be friends."

Larry pulled her back into a hug, this time loose and friendly. "Of course we can, Rosa. Of course we can."

After they'd said their final goodbye, Rosa stepped inside the mansion, closing the large wooden door behind her. The relief she felt melded with grief, and she leaned against the door, the energy to take herself upstairs and to the privacy of her room escaping her.

The loss she felt wasn't of Larry Rayburn but of the hope she'd placed in him. Stability of relationship, a future for a family with children, the next step in her life's journey. She wasn't getting any younger, and even though the term "spinster" was outdated, at twenty-eight, she was an anomaly when it came to single women. Most gals her age were already married with a car full of kids.

Rosa breathed in deeply. At least she had her career. If she ever went back to London, she could always return to the Metropolitan Police Force, and she could work in Santa Bonita indefinitely as a private investigator.

A rap on the door startled her. Had Larry come back? Rosa groaned inwardly. *One goodbye was hard enough but two? Dreadful.* She pulled open the door and gasped.

Instead of Larry's bright-blue gaze, she stared at the brooding dark eyes belonging to Miguel Belmonte.

"Oh, good," he said. "You're still here."

Feeling confused by the whole encounter, Rosa asked, "Where else would I be?"

"Do you mind if we talk? Out here?"

"Okay." Rosa stepped outside, closing the door behind her. They made it to the large three-tiered cement fountain in the middle of the circular drive, stopping on the far side where they'd be hidden from the windows. Miguel faced her, his jaw tense and eyes blazing.

"I don't want you to go with Larry."

"I'm—"

He held up a palm. "Please, let me finish. Just let me say my piece, and I'll go."

Rosa didn't dare interrupt.

"I couldn't live with myself if I didn't at least throw my hat into the ring." He inhaled as if to calm his nerves. "Ever since you came back to Santa Bonita, I've been off-kilter. I honestly never thought

I'd see you again after the war—London is another world away, and though I never stopped loving you, I had to move on. How I came to choose Charlene, I don't know, but you saved me from her. She didn't love me, and I didn't love her. I thought I did, but I didn't, not when compared to how I feel about you.

"I think about you day and night. I love working with you, and I'm so proud at how bright you are, how pretty you are, and I can't even begin to tell you how torturous it has been for me to see you with Larry Rayburn."

"Miguel—"

"No, I'm almost done. I just want to plead my case; then, if you tell me I have no hope, I'll drop it once and for all.

"I love you, Rosa. With all my being. And if you feel anything for me, at all, please don't go to Galveston."

"I'm not going to Galveston."

Miguel's head snapped up. "What?"

"I just told Larry, only moments before you came, that I didn't love him and wasn't going with him. You must've just passed him on the drive."

"I did, and I thought I was too late. I almost didn't come."

Rosa stepped toward Miguel. "I'm really glad you did."

Miguel's lips pulled up into a slow grin, and the dimples Rosa dreamed about at night made an appearance. He reached for her hand, pulled her close, tilted her chin up, and lowered his, their lips meeting.

And this time, as they kissed, Rosa most definitely felt *it*.

If you enjoyed reading *Murder at the Races* please help others enjoy it too.

Recommend it: Help others find the book by recommending it to friends, readers' groups, discussion boards and by **suggesting it to your local library.**

Review it: Please tell other readers why you liked this book by reviewing it on Amazon or Goodreads.

** Please don't add spoilers to your review. **

EAGER TO READ the next book in the Rosa Reed Mystery series?

Don't miss *Murder at the Dude Ranch* A Rosa Reed Mystery # 7.

Murder's a wild ride!

ROSA REED TAKES A MUCH NEEDED break from her thriving private investigative work by joining her cousin Clarence and Aunt Louisa for a weekend getaway at the Black Stallion Dude Ranch near Santa Bonita, California. It's the beginning of 1957 and Rosa is ready for a fresh start. Newly single, all she needs is time on the trails, and cuddles from her tabby cat, Diego.

The peace and quiet of ranch life is soon disrupted when a horse returns from a trail ride without its rider. When foul play is determined, Rosa finds herself thrust once again into a murder investigation alongside the handsome detective Miguel Belmonte.

Suspicion falls on many of the guests— the failed investment banker, the laundromat owner, the heiress, and to Rosa's dismay, her own cousin Clarence.

Can Rosa prove her cousin's innocence before the cows come home?

NOTE FROM THE AUTHORS
HISTORY OF STOCK CAR RACING

The early history of stock car racing is replete with colorful characters, accounts of modified cars, and middle of the night police chases through the Appalachian Mountains featuring death-defying feats of acrobatic driving. The connection between the sport and the bootleg industry is well documented and provides a backdrop for this story.

Inspiration for the Downing brothers characters came from a real life family. The 'Flock Gang', from Alabama was comprised of nine siblings, four of which were involved in racing. Tim, Fonty, Bob and their sister Ethel were all prominent professional drivers in the late 40's and into the 50's. Their sister Reo Flock was a noted wing-walker, barnstormer, stunt performer and champion skeet shooter. Their father Carl Lee Flock, a cab driver in Fort Payne, was a local celebrity who entertained people as a bicycle racer, trick cyclist, and tightrope walker.

They were quite a family.

Of further note, Tim Flock was the only NASCAR driver to race with a monkey in the car. Yes, that's right, a monkey. His partner was a rhesus monkey name 'Jocko Flock' (which is a bit of a mouthful). The two managed to win one major race together as well as several second, third and fourth titles before Jocko went crazy one day after being hit in the head by a stray rock and had to be removed from the car during a pit stop.

The idea of a NASCAR driver breaking through the barricade and leading the police on a chase might seem far fetched, but there is the story from the late 40's where Bob Flock, banned from a race because of his criminal record, snuck into a race at Atlanta's Lakewood Speedway wearing a bandana. When the police tried to arrest him he led them on a chase around the speedway, through the fence and into the streets of the city.

As the saying goes, "You can't make this stuff up."

ABOUT THE AUTHORS

Lee Strauss is a USA TODAY bestselling author of The Ginger Gold Mysteries series, The Higgins & Hawke Mystery series, The Rosa Reed Mystery series (cozy historical mysteries), A Nursery Rhyme Mystery series (mystery suspense), The Perception series (young adult dystopian), The Light & Love series (sweet romance), The Clockwise Collection (YA time travel romance), and young adult historical fiction with over a million books read. She has titles published in German, Spanish and Korean, and a growing audio library.

When Lee's not writing or reading she likes to cycle, hike, and watch the ocean. She loves to drink caffè lattes and red wines in exotic places, and eat dark chocolate anywhere.

Norm Strauss is a singer-songwriter and performing artist who's seen the stage of The Voice of Germany. Cozy mystery writing is a new passion he shares with his wife Lee Strauss. Check out Norm's music page www.normstrauss.com

For more info on books by Lee Strauss and her social media links, visit leestraussbooks.com. To make sure you don't miss the next new release, be sure to sign up for her readers' list!

Did you know you can follow your favorite authors on Bookbub? If you subscribe to Bookbub — (and if you don't, why don't you? - They'll send you daily emails alerting you to sales and new releases on just the kind of books you like to read!) — follow me to make sure you don't miss the next Ginger Gold Mystery!

www.leestraussbooks.com

leestraussbooks@gmail.com

MORE FROM LEE STRAUSS

On AMAZON

THE ROSA REED MYSTERIES

(1950s cozy historical)

Murder at High Tide

Murder on the Boardwalk

Murder at the Bomb Shelter

Murder on Location

Murder and Rock 'n' Roll

Murder at the Races

Murder at the Dude Ranch

Murder in London

GINGER GOLD MYSTERY SERIES (cozy 1920s historical)

Cozy. Charming. Filled with Bright Young Things. This Jazz Age murder mystery will entertain and delight you with its 1920s flair and pizzazz!

Murder on the SS Rosa

Murder at Hartigan House

Murder at Bray Manor

Murder at Feathers & Flair

Murder at the Mortuary

Murder at Kensington Gardens

Murder at St. George's Church

The Wedding of Ginger & Basil

Murder Aboard the Flying Scotsman

Murder at the Boat Club

Murder on Eaton Square

Murder by Plum Pudding

Murder on Fleet Street

Murder at Brighton Beach

Murder in Hyde Park

Murder at the Royal Albert Hall

Murder in Belgravia

LADY GOLD INVESTIGATES (Ginger Gold companion short stories)

Volume 1

Volume 2

Volume 3

Volume 4

HIGGINS & HAWKE MYSTERY SERIES (cozy 1930s historical)

The 1930s meets Rizzoli & Isles in this friendship depression era cozy mystery series.

Death at the Tavern

Death on the Tower

Death on Hanover

A NURSERY RHYME MYSTERY SERIES(mystery/sci fi)

Marlow finds himself teamed up with intelligent and savvy Sage Farrell, a girl so far out of his league he feels blinded in her presence - literally - damned glasses! Together they work to find the identity of @gingerbreadman. Can they stop the killer before he strikes again?

Gingerbread Man

Life Is but a Dream

Hickory Dickory Dock

Twinkle Little Star

THE PERCEPTION TRILOGY (YA dystopian mystery)

Zoe Vanderveen is a GAP—a genetically altered person. She lives in the security of a walled city on prime water-front property alongside other equally beautiful people with extended life spans. Her brother Liam is missing. Noah Brody, a boy on the outside, is the only one who can help ~ but can she trust him?

Perception

Volition

Contrition

LIGHT & LOVE (sweet romance)

Set in the dazzling charm of Europe, follow Katja, Gabriella, Eva, Anna and Belle as they find strength, hope and love.

Sing me a Love Song

Your Love is Sweet

In Light of Us

Lying in Starlight

PLAYING WITH MATCHES (WW2 history/romance)

A sobering but hopeful journey about how one young German boy copes with the war and propaganda. Based on true events.

A Piece of Blue String (companion short story)

THE CLOCKWISE COLLECTION (YA time travel romance)

Casey Donovan has issues: hair, height and uncontrollable trips to the 19th century! And now this ~ she's accidentally taken Nate Mackenzie, the cutest boy in the school, back in time. Awkward.

Clockwise

Clockwiser

Like Clockwork

Counter Clockwise

Clockwork Crazy

Clocked (companion novella)

Standalones

Seaweed

Love, Tink

www.ingramcontent.com/pod-product-compliance
Lightning Source LLC
Chambersburg PA
CBHW050255110726
47898CB00007B/2423

9 7 8 1 7 7 4 0 9 1 4 1 8